the Wild Rover

RICHARD COLESHAW

Illustrations by David Riding

First published by Richard Coleshaw, 2023

Copyright © 2023 Richard Coleshaw

ISBN | 978-0-7961-0163-1 | Print
ISBN | 978-0-7961-0164-8 | eBook

Illustrations by David Riding

Cover Design and Typesetting
by www.myebook.online

Cousins David Riding and Richard Coleshaw grew up in what used to be Rhodesia at a time when the human population of that country was about a quarter of what it is now. And the wild animal population was about four times what it is to-day.

David's parents were part owners of a funny old hotel close to the Wankie Game Reserve, so the two youngsters spent many happy, really close-up times, with wild animals both big and small. This led to a love of wildlife and – in their later years – a great sadness at its steady demise.

1

I had been expecting the call.

"Is that Mr Shirley"?

No cheery "Hello Denis;" not even a more formal "Good morning Mr. Shirley".

Let's get right down to business.

"Is that Mr. Shirley"?

No point in denying it. I recognised the voice. It had come to be known as The Voice of Death. It was an official sort of voice, crisp and authoritative, and it belonged to Ms. Rita Blake, the Personal Assistant of Mr. Henry Baldwin, the new Managing Director of my company.

"Mr. Baldwin would like to see you in his office. Ten 'o' clock to-morrow".

No question of my availability – when Mr. Baldwin wanted to see someone, the call had to be obeyed. Cancel all other meetings.

My company had recently merged with one of our major competitors. While a merger of the two companies made a lot of sense – both marketed much the same products through much the same distribution channels – the cultures of the two entities were very different. In my company, the atmosphere tended to be relaxed and informal; we worked hard but we sometimes managed to have a little fun. Baldwin, on the other hand, had run his company along strictly military lines. Fun – and any sort of familiarity - was frowned upon. I had spent much of the last twenty years trying to outmanoeuvre – sometimes by fair means but not infrequently by foul – Baldwin's company and it was rather unfortunate that the man was now my boss.

Mr. Baldwin was one of those people who wore a permanently mournful, disapproving expression on his face and I had given him what I felt was an entirely appropriate soubriquet. The Undertaker. I realised that he was probably aware of the title – and that he knew where it had originated.

"Let's see….." I said, pretending to consult my diary. I could almost hear the irritation at the other end of the line. "Let's see. Uhmm. Ten 'o' clock to-morrow?" A suitable pause. "Yes….yes… I think I can make it. See you then Rita".

Rita. I knew that this inappropriate familiarity would not go down well with Ms Blake —she was, after all, the Personal Assistant to the Managing Director. I wondered if anyone in the company – apart from, (at the Christmas party), her boss - had ever called her Rita before.

I had a very good idea why Baldwin wanted to see me. The talks of a merger had been on-going for several months. Then came the news that it was to go ahead. Huge savings would be made. Efficiency would improve unrecognisably. Profits would double – nay, treble. Of course, jobs would be lost – that was inevitable. But in an increasingly competitive business climate, that was often the price that had to be paid, wasn't it? And besides all that – mergers were quite fashionable these days.

So, I guessed, Baldwin would explain to me that times were tough, that drastic measures would have to be taken to save the company. That, heartbreaking though it was, there was no alternative but to let some people go. Good way of putting it – "to let someone go". As though the person was some sort of animal that had for long been caged against its will and was now to be given its freedom.

I gazed gloomily out of the window of my office. It can be very hot in Cape Town in January, but to-day it was cool – with a chance of rain. Table Mountain brooded over the city but its familiar "tablecloth", the clouds created by the south-easter, was absent. No doubt the hordes of tourists that flocked to South Africa's Mother City would be queuing to take the cable car up to the top of the mountain. A good day to "do" the mountain.

Though the term "taking early retirement" had a certain prestigious ring to it - especially if one could add in an off-hand manner some comment about there being no real need to continue working - for me, being out of a job at age forty-six was not an attractive proposition. I had a strong feeling that I was going to sorely miss that salary cheque on the 25th of every month.

The company had recently arranged for presentations from immaculately dressed and very bright whiz kids from a financial services institution and we had been given an idea of how much money one needed, at retirement age, to go off and do the fishing/golfing thing. According to my calculations, I would not be able to retire much before age 119. So I knew that I would have to find something else to do and I also knew that the world of commerce was not exactly desperate for forty-six year old marketing executives. Especially those who had been let go. Highflyers are not usually retrenched.

At least, I consoled myself, my financial commitments were not that excessive. Two years ago, I had parted with a significant portion of my modest assets to satisfy my now ex-wife and her hyena offspring divorce lawyer but I had just about recovered from that setback. The mortgage I had on my small townhouse in central Cape Town was not too much of a burden. And my only child, a daughter, was in her final year at Cape Town University. She was a bright girl and hard working and I was pretty confident that she would graduate come the end of the year. Her plan was then to spend a couple of years working her way around Europe and I hoped that I would be asked to contribute little more than a return airline ticket. Further, the early retirement settlements the company was giving, seemed fair enough. So I was, I had to admit, in a better position than some of my recently released colleagues who still had salary devouring school-going children and hefty mortgage commitments.

But redundancy had never been part of my long-term career plans. It had been almost twenty years since, clad in my best suit and sporting a new shirt and tie, I had set off for an interview for a junior position in the marketing department of the company. Determined and brimming with confidence. With a couple of years experience behind me, I reckoned I knew just about every-thing there was to be known about the marketing discipline and I was certain that I would be an irresistible prospect for any consumer goods company. As the years went by I had made my way up the ladder steadily enough, eventually ending up on the board of directors having gathered along the way good experience of how not to do things. But I had not reckoned on what I thought was almost certainly going to be a career change right now.

* * *

I waited gloomily in Ms Blake's office the following day. Ms Blake was hunched over her keyboard doing her best to look severe. Working no doubt on some document of critical importance to the company. Or perhaps it was a letter setting out the details of my severance package. Her small mouth was set in a prim, grave line; there was an official looking furrow on her forehead.

I wondered if the rumours of an affair with the MD had any substance. It seemed unlikely to me – though one look at Baldwin's powerfully built wife, dressed in her favourite battleship gray, dispensing largesse and barking like a Rottweiler at industry get-togethers, would add credence to the proposition. But somehow, I couldn't imagine Baldwin "in flagrante delicto" with Ms Blake. Especially not under the watchful eye of a block mounted water-colour portrait of a female wearing a grotesque grin hanging on the wall behind Ms Blake's desk. "My Mom" it was titled. "By Jennifer. 6". Lone evidence of a human side to Ms Blake but no early signs of artistic talent in the portrait.

A buzzer sounded and Ms Blake cocked her head in an efficient, alert sort of way.

"You may go through now, Mr. Shirley", she said crisply, her eyes never moving from the all-important screen.

"Thanks Rita", I said as I walked past her desk. Another tiny victory.

"Ah Desmond", said Baldwin managing a small smile and striding forward with his hand outstretched. Now that we were, for a few minutes at least, part of the same company, this sort of relaxed informality was allowed.

"It's Denis", I said, firmly returning his rather limp handshake.

"Tch – of course it is", he agreed. How silly of him.

Unusually, Baldwin was in almost jovial spirits. "Sit down Denis", gesturing expansively towards the chairs in a corner of his large office. "Let's sit here – we'll be more comfortable than at that damned desk". The Last Meal of the Condemned Man theme. Get the bullet in the leather chair.

How to begin?

Baldwin donned a more familiar lugubrious look. He removed his spectacles and rubbed his temples with his fingertips. His eyes closed, he gave a sorrowful sigh.

"As you know Desmond… ah…. Denis, these are rather difficult times", he began.

"And as a result, the shareholders and I have had to make some difficult decisions". A pause. "Some very difficult decisions", Baldwin emphasised.

Another pause.

I wondered if he was rather enjoying the meeting.

"In fact…uh… Desmond, these have… probably been… the most challenging times I have been through in my professional career", he revealed frankly, looking even more sorrowful than usual.

I did my best to put on an expression of sympathy and compassion.

"Unfortunately, we have had to cut back on expenses – examine every area where savings could be made".

Except, perhaps, in vehicle purchasing I thought, having on several occasions admired the new top of the range Mercedes parked in Baldwin's personal garage.

"As you would know Desmond…tch…Denis" (as a senior executive, I would, of course, be privy to such confidential information), "personnel expenses account for around 60% of total overheads. And my colleagues and I had no alternative, therefore, but to take a very hard look at that area".

It made sense.

"We reached the conclusion Desmond, that, unfortunately, we had no choice but to let some of our employees go".

I know. I had watched several of my friends bounding off across the plains to freedom in the last couple of weeks.

"I'm afraid, Desmond, in the end – and taking all factors into consideration - we have reluctantly decided ….. that there is no longer a place for you in the company".

Looking straight into my eyes with an expression of great sympathy and sincerity.

Not much I can say is there?

"We have, however, gone right to the limit to ensure that those who leave us take with them a just and fair reward for their services", Baldwin added hastily.

"I think you'll agree that we've done rather well", allowing himself a small, triumphant smile, "despite certain objections from the shareholders". A note of defiance in his voice.

Can't really comment on that one until I see the numbers.

Baldwin rose to his feet and proffered his hand.

"I'd like to wish you everything of the best Desmond", he said as warmly as possible. "You're a very capable manager" (that's why we let you go) "and you'll probably have no difficulty in finding another position. Possibly," he added with a short bark, "an even better one!!" An unsuccessful attempt to be jocular.

"Ms Blake has a letter for you setting out the details of your package".

Crisply.

I didn't ask Baldwin if he had any suggestions as to where I might start looking for this possibly better position as I left his office. With economic conditions in South Africa as difficult as they were, he knew as well as I did that the chances of my finding a position similar to, let alone better than, the one I had just lost were remote.

"I believe you have something for me?" I asked Ms Blake.

"Ah.....yes" she said. For a moment I couldn't quite think what you were talking about. Your severance letter. Oh yes - it just happens to be right here next to my computer. A rather smug expression on her face.

I thought fleetingly of telling Rita how much I was going to miss her but decided against it.

* * *

So now it was my turn to clear my desk; to say good-bye to colleagues. My turn to send off a few farewell notes to the people I had worked with, explaining that I was another victim of merger mania. Written on my own note paper, titled - From the Desk of Denis Shirley. Not from Denis Shirley himself, but from his desk. Well, there would be no more memos or messages – not from Denis Shirley or from his desk.

2

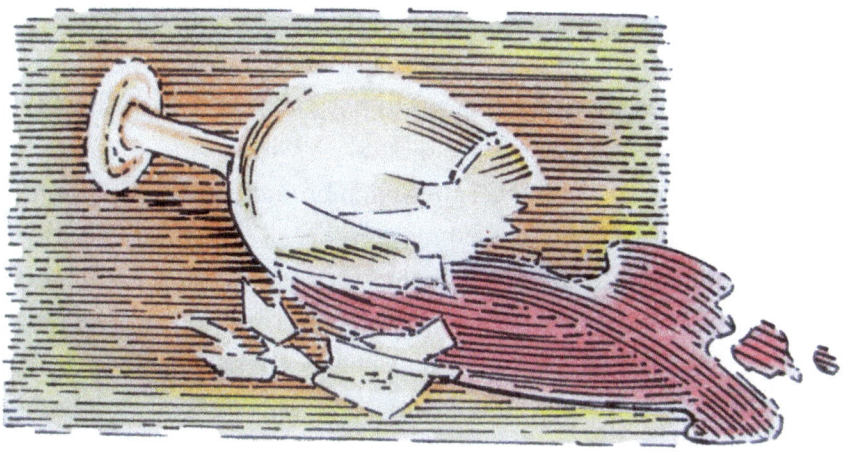

"Probably a blessing in disguise", said Anton.

A handful of newly released and a couple of still captive employees had met in our favourite pub in Cape Town to discuss the future of the company, the economy, the political situation and, later, the meaning of life and mankind and womankind in general. As the wine flowed and the evening progressed the solutions to all these conundrums became ever more creative.

Anton Barnard was an old friend. We had joined the company at about the same time when Anton's feelings of infinite superiority had been every bit the equal of mine. We had no doubt, at that stage, that we would take the art of marketing to previously undreamed of heights - that at last there had come to the discipline, two people of rare and wonderful talent.

We hadn't been entirely correct in that assessment but we had worked hard and we had managed to have a great deal of fun along the way. Our tales of the good old days, growing in the telling in the soft lights in the pub had, over the years, brought whistles of amazement and disbelief from new employees.

"I'm not sure the merger is going to work", Anton commented gloomily. "The cultures of the two companies are just too different." He looked after the company's small statistics department; there was no-one with whom he could be merged, so Baldwin had not let him go.

"At least you have a fairly decent package", Anton pointed out. "It could be worse." After helping himself to another glass of Shiraz.

"Any thoughts on what you might do?"

I gazed deeply into the garnet-coloured liquid in my glass.

Someone famous had once suggested that there were no problems, only opportunities. After the better part of a bottle of good Cape wine I was beginning to see a deeper meaning in the proposition - it was starting to take on ever more credence. Now that the company had let me go - now that I was free - the possibilities seemed endless.

"You know what I've always wanted to do?" I asked, gazing sincerely at Anton. A mood of courage and defiance was steadily creeping over me.

Anton confessed that he didn't.

"I've lived all my life in southern Africa", I revealed to Anton.

"And yet", I continued, nodding my head slowly and with a far-off look in my eyes, "and yet…. there are places in this part of the world that I have never seen. Many places". A shameful admission.

"I don't mean your topless beaches and your casinos here", I hastened to tell Anton. "I'm talking about….. The Real Africa".

"South Africa has one of the richest eco systems in the world". I was lecturing now. "We have more plant and animal species than any other continent". I wasn't one hundred per cent sure that this claim was true but the statement had an impressive ring to it.

I paused, to let this information sink in.

"I've always wanted to get off the beaten track", I explained earnestly. "Really off the beaten track", I repeated, my eyes narrowed dangerously.

"I'm not talking about those ten-star luxury bush camps where the animals are brought out to parade in front of camera clicking millionaires". There was more than a hint of scorn in my voice. Such places would, of course, be beyond the means of the freshly unemployed.

"Know what I'm going to do?" I asked again, pouring another glass of Shiraz.

Anton waited breathlessly.

"I'm going to get hold of an old 4 x 4". I informed him. "Something I can convert into a camper. Go where I want to go. Stay for as long as I like. Something I should have done years ago", I confessed, shaking my head regretfully. Only then I had a job.

"What do you have in mind?" Anton asked politely.

I considered the question carefully.

"Probably an old Landie", I mused thoughtfully. "Simple machines, easy to fix. Go anywhere". And not beyond the modest means of someone who has just been released from his job.

Anton looked at me doubtfully.

"Do you... know much about old Land Rovers?" he asked tactfully.

It was a good question. We had been friends for long enough for Anton to know that my knowledge of things mechanical was not far from zero.

"An old one can be quite temperamental, you know", Anton continued.

"You don't want to be stuck out in the middle of nowhere with a breakdown – especially if you're all alone".

I couldn't deny that he had a point.

"I could learn", I countered defensively. "They have those mechanic courses at the technical college", I pointed out. "I could do one of those courses; learn enough to renovate an old Landie". I knew it sounded a bit vague, but right now, nothing was impossible.

"Where would you go?" Anton had decided to humour me. "Not to the ten-star places or the topless beaches", he added hastily.

There was a calm, distant look in my eyes. I could see a new me – relaxed, totally at peace with the world. Instead of a suit and tie I would be clad in clothing that blended perfectly with the outdoors. An unshaven jowl. Place names like San-ta-Wani, Pandamatenga, Thamalakane, Selebi Pikwe, would roll effortlessly off my tongue. No more hassles from Baldwin and the bottom line. There I would be - telling anyone who would listen that I should have made the move years ago. At this stage, the financial aspects seemed unimportant - irrelevant really.

"There's so much to see in southern Africa, Anton. But it's disappearing fast", I cautioned earnestly. "I want to visit the unspoiled parts of this country, while they're still very much the way they were hundreds of years ago. I want to get close to Nature - see nothing but bush for miles and miles".

I gestured expansively, sending Anton's glass crashing to the floor.

The plan called for another bottle of Shiraz and a new glass for Anton.

"I could be ready by mid-year", I informed him, warming to my theme. Winter in the highveld. The perfect time to set off. Enough time to find a Landie and kit it out for camping.

Fortified by the good wine, I was able to speak with some authority on these matters. I had, after all, done a bit of camping in my time; I had owned a small caravan at one stage and also an old 4 x 4 truck in which my daughter and I had spent many enjoyable days off road. But never for any length of time – I had always to hurry back to deal with an out-of-stock problem here, a loss of market share there.

So it was not surprising that when life in the office had been particularly stressful I had gazed out of my window, imagining how I would one day put together my dream safari vehicle and set off defiantly for the wilds - to go wherever I wanted and to stay there for as long as I wished. Sitting there in the pub, my freedom granted, the severance cheque freshly banked, I was convinced that the time had come.

The way ahead was clear. It was simple. I would find an old Land Rover. I knew a guy who owned a garage that specialised in such vehicles. He would help me – point me in the right direction. I would work with one of his mechanics on the restoration project – learning as we went along. I would join the Land Rover Club – pick up a few tips, go on a couple of outings. Then I would sally forth, knowing everything about Land Rovers, the wilderness, Nature - and Life itself. The more I thought about it, the more sense it made. As Anton had said, my dismissal had been a blessing in disguise.

I finished my wine, pushed the glass away from me. There was work to be done, arrangements to be made. The better part of two bottles of good Shiraz had greatly assisted in bringing me to that conclusion.

I stood up uncertainly, shook Anton's hand. He wished me well and we promised to meet regularly – to reminisce on what had just become the Good Old Days.

I could hear the Wilderness softly calling.

3

"One door closes, another one opens".

If I hear that pearl of wisdom once more, I thought, I am going to be sick.

As I had feared, my efforts to find another job were not meeting with a great deal of success. I had spent a couple of days sitting at home calling up old friends and acquaintances, to ask if they knew of any openings for someone with my experience. I had even tried one or two head-hunters. But all the doors at which I knocked - if they were not immediately slammed shut in my face - remained firmly closed. No new doors opened and the sympathy and words of encouragement only made the situation worse. It was a distressing experience for one who, not that long ago, had seen himself as a marketing legend in the making.

In the past few years, as economic conditions in South Africa had become more difficult, I had received a number of calls similar to those I was now making.

"Hello Denis? Chris Alberts here. We were at junior school together. You nearly took my head off with a hockey stick during one match – you must remember?"

Unfortunately, I didn't. And Chris must have been getting dangerously close to the bottom of his barrel of contacts if he was phoning to remind me of an incident that had taken place about forty years ago so that he could enquire if I knew of any jobs going.

"I've just been made redundant", the story would go "and I was wondering if there was anything going in your company?"

"Afraid not," I would reply. "But I wish you everything of the best."

And I hope and pray that I will never be in your position.

But now I was. It was discouraging and depressing – trying to sound relaxed and upbeat when asking for a job and, when nothing was available, to agree wholeheartedly that another door would, at any moment, swing open.

I thought back to my conversation with Anton on the night of my farewell party. After several glasses of good red wine the idea of setting off bravely into the wilds in an elderly but beautifully restored Land Rover had seemed a splendid counter to my unfortunate dismissal – and a relatively straightforward undertaking. True, the proposition had become a little more complicated the next morning when I had awoken, feeling quite some distance from the top of the world. But was the idea really feasible?

Certainly, the dream was not impossible. Well matured Land Rovers were available – and if one could find a sound specimen, fixing it up should not prove ruinously expensive. Especially if I could play some part in the restoration and do some of the donkey work myself, learning as I went along.

I thought about the financial implications. I could probably afford the cost of buying and renovating an old vehicle and if I was thrifty, I could survive for several months without any income. It would also be satisfying to prove Anton's scepticism wrong. And I certainly didn't feel like making any more phone calls to friends and employment agents in the hope that - right behind the next door - would be a wonderful opportunity for someone just like me. I had long loved the bush and yearned to escape to it for more than just a few hurried days. Perhaps the merger really had provided me with the opportunity?

A sensible starting point would be an accurate estimate of the cost of the rig I had in mind. I decided I might as well take a drive out to my friend at his Land Rover garage without further delay.

The call of the Wilderness was getting louder.

* * *

Hidden amidst the factories in an unfashionable part of Cape Town's industrial area, it was clear that not a great deal of effort had gone into making the garage look attractive. No gardens or fountains or vast showroom windows with chrome frames. A wooden sign with the name of the garage and the faded remains of the Land Rover oval. A badly scarred, ill-tempered looking dog patrolling a securely fenced yard filled with Land Rovers of all ages in various stages of undress. In the service bay a couple of Defenders, almost completely concealed by roof top tents, rows of spotlights, gas bottles, shovels and spare wheels. Back windows obliterated by stickers proving that the most inaccessible corners of southern Africa had been conquered. Behind the wheel of such a vehicle any man or woman would instantly become a celebrity. In one corner a new Range Rover Vogue, its leather first class aircraft type seats and mirror-like paint finish strangely incongruous in this environment. It struggled to conceal its disdain for its bottom of the range, entry level, work horse cousins.

A bell fastened to the top of the door sounded a warning as I entered the office. Two yesteryear desks. In-baskets that had seemingly lain undisturbed for years. On the walls, faded advertisements for early Land Rovers. Photos of Land Rovers up to their axles in mud; Land Rovers clawing their way up almost vertical slopes. A Land Rover that had for some reason been driven into the middle of a lake. A three-year old calendar with a bikini bursting model advertising ball bearings.

Trevor emerged from a side door, wiping his hands on a cloth that might once have been white. A lined, tanned face, grey flecks creeping into the short hair around the temples. A strong, wiry body. The relaxed demeanour of a man for whom a breakdown in the remotest corner of the darkest wilderness would hold no fears. A cheery grin greeted he whose obvious ignorance of the arcane workings of the four-wheel drive system was a subject of benign amusement.

I accepted the offer of a cold Coke and seated myself gingerly on the edge of a battered sofa. Carefully, I outlined my scheme. To find an old Land Rover, renovate it, then set off into the wilds to fulfil a lifelong dream. All the while peering earnestly at Trevor while trying to sound as though I was in familiar territory. Probably the old Series II, I mused. The two door, pick-up model, with space behind the seats for living quarters. I would, of course, need long range tanks and some sort of container for fresh water. Trevor would understand that. And probably a Salisbury diff would be a good idea, I ventured. Hoping that he wouldn't ask me why as I wasn't altogether sure of the benefits of a Salisbury diff. But I had listened once to a couple of Land Rover buffs discussing its merits and it seemed like a good thing to have. Could he, I enquired, give me any indication of the cost of the endeavour? And, with a little cough, if I could find the right vehicle, would it be at all possible for me to be involved in the restoration process? All the while keeping my eyes steadfastly averted from a yellowing sign on the wall behind Trevor's desk. A sign that read –

Our Rates Are R250.00 per hour

R280.00 if you watch

R300.00 if you help

There was a good-natured twinkle in Trevor's eyes. Of course it could be done – and no, if we were careful, it shouldn't cost too much. Nor did he envisage any problem with my working with one of his mechanics in the renovation process. Though I thought I detected a hint of a mischievous smile on Trevor's face when he agreed to this request. What was more, Trevor had heard of a Series 11 on a used vehicle stand not far from his garage, though he had not been to have a look at it and had no idea of its condition.

I determined to pay the dealer a visit without delay - there was no time to lose.

The Wilderness was beginning to send urgent calls for my presence.

* * *

I found the dealer without difficulty. Uncle Ben's Used Cars. It was not the sort of place you would visit if you were looking for a late model Aston Martin or Jaguar. Several rows of once in a lifetime opportunities, gifts and bargains. Lurking in the back row I spotted the unmistakable box-like profile of a Land Rover. I parked outside the gate and threaded my way through Ben's irresistible offers, hoping to have the opportunity to examine the vehicle in peace.

No such luck. Uncle Ben zeroed in on me the moment I entered his domain and hurriedly stubbing out his cigarette slithered out of his office. I imagined a shark's fin gliding towards me through the rows of never to be repeated opportunities.

"Best model Land Rover ever made", proclaimed Uncle Ben, hoisting one foot onto the front bumper. A heavy gold chain glinted around his neck. "Very difficult to find one in this sort of condition nowadays", he added. "Very difficult". I wondered if he was going to continue with the-old-lady-who-used-the-car-only-for-church-on-Sundays line.

At first glance, the vehicle looked like it might be a proposition. It was the two-door pick-up version that I was hoping to find and I could see no signs of accident damage. Clearly, it required work in certain areas but as it was my intention to rebuild it entirely, this should not be a problem.

Uncle Ben's sales pitch was warming up. "I wouldn't touch the new Land Rover", he revealed. "Far too complex. Far too complex. You're out in the desert and you have a break-down in one of those things and they have to fly in a technician with a computer". He chortled derisively. "Give me one of these old babies every time" he went on, gazing admiringly at the old vehicle. While Ben didn't strike me as the sort of person who spent a lot of time out in the desert, the voice of authority had spoken. Though I strongly suspected that had he been selling me a late model Land Rover, his scorn would have been directed at the older baby. Far too primitive. Far too primitive.

I asked Uncle Ben if I could take the Land Rover for a test drive and his response was generous; clearly Ben operated in an environment of trust and integrity. It would be his pleasure he assured me expansively. Any test I wanted. Remembering, of course, that this was an old vehicle and one could not expect too much from it.

I swung open the wide door, hoisted myself onto the Spartan seat behind that large plastic steering wheel. Swung it from side to side to indicate subtly to Uncle Ben that there was rather too much play in the mechanism. Remembering that the starter button on these older models was hidden below the dashboard. A psychological advantage would be lost if I had to ask Uncle Ben how to start the engine.

It had been many years since I had driven an older Land Rover - way back in my army service days. Then, the aim of all the recruits was to exact revenge not only on the training sergeants and the officers but on the entire military system by doing one's best to destroy army property – vehicles in particular. See how fast this baby can travel through thick bush! See how it knocks down trees! The Land Rovers, however, earned grudging admiration and a great deal of affection by defying most attempts to destroy them.

It wasn't long before I was back with Trevor. His eyes ran over the old vehicle. "Let me give Fred a call", he said.

A figure in brown overalls emerged scowling from the dark recesses of the workshop. At some time, I guessed, Fred would have played in the front row of one of the local rugby teams. Never would a collar be buttoned around that neck. With his barrel chest and powerful arms, Fred could probably lift an engine block out of a truck without too much difficulty. Even though, judging by his waistline, Fred had been a little neglectful in the keep fit department since hanging up his rugby boots.

"Mr. Shirley is looking at buying this Series 11", said Trevor by way of introduction. Taking no notice of Mr. Shirley, Fred stalked around the vehicle. I hoped he wouldn't kick any of the tyres. He opened the bonnet, peered inside the engine bay then lay down on the ground and wriggled ponderously under the engine. Respectfully, I leaned down to witness the examination. Fred seemed to be doing his best to break something off the engine and I wondered how I would explain the damage to Uncle Ben.

Eventually, he emerged from under the vehicle, rubbing his hands on an old cloth. The back of his head was covered in dust and small leaves but he didn't bother to brush them away. I was glad that he had not called me down to the ground to point out some problem with the mechanics. I couldn't imagine myself wriggling in the dust in my almost new Polo shirt.

"Mr. Shirley is wanting to have the vehicle renovated", Trevor explained to Fred. "Overhaul the engine and gearbox, suspension and electrics. Trevor smiled encouragingly at me. "And he wants to be involved in the work".

Fred looked less than pleased with this proposition. Glaring balefully at Trevor, he asked "how much?"

"Forty-five thousand", I stated cautiously, hoping that Fred would not burst out laughing.

"Tell him thirty", he told Trevor, retiring into his workshop.

Feeling both excited and nervous, I drove back to Uncle Ben's, noting that the petrol gauge was flickering fitfully on E. Ben obviously didn't believe that a long test drive was necessary.

Remember to exercise care and patience when changing gear – double de-clutching I think they used to call it. And selecting reverse gear required a certain cunning. Allow a bit of extra stopping distance when braking. Allow several hundred metres if you want to do a U turn. Bouncing along on the rigid suspension, staring out over the spare wheel fixed to the bonnet. Gazing down on lesser mortals as we waited at traffic lights. With hindsight, thinking that I shouldn't have shaved this morning.

"What do you think?" I asked the Land Rover, flicking on the indicators. The horn worked, as did the windscreen wipers, though it was difficult to imagine them coping with anything more challenging than a heavy dew. "Could we become partners?" I asked. Although showing signs of its age, the vehicle had a solid enough feel and it seemed that it had not been badly treated during its Sunday drives with the old lady. I decided I rather liked it.

"I'll give you thirty", I informed Uncle Ben.

Ben winced and spread apart his arms beseechingly. "Please!! These vehicles are becoming collector's items", he countered, with just a hint of a whine in his voice. And, he disclosed, it was …how many years since he last had one on his stand? Ben couldn't remember now - but wow! - it had been a very long time.

I had never been much good at the bargaining thing. Couldn't countenance Ben and I haggling over the price in his little wooden hut. I pointed out to Ben that there were several areas where attention was required and reminded him that repairs were no longer inexpensive. What was his bottom line? Ben gazed lovingly at the truck, rubbed his jowl. "Let's split the difference", he suggested magnanimously. "I'll let it go for forty". Maths had evidently not been Ben's strong point at school.

Silently resolving not to mention this figure to Fred, I signed the papers and arranged to collect the vehicle the following day.

* * *

Driving back to my townhouse, I was, of course, filled with remorse.

What I had just done was highly irresponsible! I should be ploughing on with the hunt for another job – there was no way I was in a position to take an indefinite holiday! I could, I supposed, call Uncle Ben and tell him the deal was off. Being Uncle Ben, I was sure he would understand. Give Trevor a vague story about the time not being right. Confirm Fred's certain view that I was an un-rehabilitated office nerd.

No, I thought to myself. I have started on this journey and I am going to finish it. And perish the consequences.

To reinforce this bold decision, I called in at the co-op store and bought myself a pair of overalls. The first time in my life that I had owned a garment of this nature. I chose a dark blue colour, rather than Fred's more practical brown. In subtle harmony with the blue overalls, I invested in a pair of sturdy dark brown shoes with high ankle supports and soles that resembled the tread on the tyre of a large truck. The kind of shoes that were popular with farmers. I wondered if Fred would be able to conceal his contempt when I arrived in my brand new ensemble. Probably not, but if I was to enter a new world, one in which grinding crankshafts and skimming heads was a daily task, I had to be appropriately attired.

I called Trevor, told him I was happy with the price I had paid and we agreed that I would present myself and my new acquisition on Monday next week. I would be wearing my brand new overalls and shoes. The project was underway; my aim was to be on the road by June.

The Wilderness was now bellowing for my presence.

I had though, to consider carefully the way forward. Fred had given the very distinct impression that the prospect of my working with him on the restoration of the vehicle did not hold much appeal. Clearly, he did not think highly of white-collar managers who could not renovate their own vehicles. I imagined him issuing curt instructions in the esoteric language of the workshop. Hand me a five-eighths; clean that rocker; replace that ball joint. And I guessed that he would probably not show much patience when I asked him what a five-eighths was and where one might start searching for a rocker. Or a ball joint. Or any of the other things that make a vehicle work. And how does one go about grinding a crankshaft?

Further, I had no clear idea of what rebuilding really meant. I had heard people talk of "completely rebuilding" a vehicle, but I wasn't sure what exactly it entailed. Taking the thing apart and putting it together again, I supposed. Replacing or repairing all worn or broken parts in the process. Clearly, I was in for a tough time in the workshop and I was going to have to do my best to learn rather quickly.

I did though, have a good idea of how I wanted to equip the vehicle in terms of it being my home for a few weeks. Cupboards and a bed in the back, together with a small fridge that drew power from a heavy duty battery. Chilled wine perfectly complements African sunsets. A roof top tent for warm nights with a platform on which I could sit sipping the wine as the sun went down and the animals came out to parade dutifully before me. I could see it all working perfectly when I was gazing out of my office window. And no doubt I would pick up even better ideas when I joined the Land Rover club.

Several days after the project had begun, I learned that Fred did have a sense of humour; that the permanent frown on his brown walnut like face would occasionally disappear fleetingly. I had been wrestling with a particularly obstinate nut when the spanner had slipped and I had taken off what looked like nearly all of the skin on two of the knuckles on my right hand. Though he didn't laugh out loud, I could see that Fred keenly appreciated the hilarity of the incident. But perhaps I had been through some sort of initiation ritual, because Fred became a little more approachable from that day on.

My Land Rover was by then in several hundred parts scattered around a far corner of the workshop. Every evening I had returned home and spent quite a while cleaning the dirt and grease off my hands before recording the details of the day's work on my computer. I had by now made myself familiar with most of the parts that would contribute towards taking me across the backroads of southern Africa and I was, thankfully, having to ask Fred fewer and fewer questions. Moreover, after a couple of trips to the laundromat, my overalls had lost their crisp new character – they had also acquired a number of permanent stains. The farmer type shoes were suitably scuffed. The proud badges of rank of those who knew their way around garages.

Progress was slow but steady. The engine, the gearbox, the suspension. The wiring for all the electrics. The body-work, in several pieces, had been sent off to a spray painter, as had the chassis. New tyres awaited the freshly painted wheels. Measurements had been taken for the folding tent for the roof and a sturdy ladder had been made for access to this haven. A water tank had been manufactured; provision made for a small brass tap to be cunningly concealed on the outside of the vehicle beside the back door. I had stolen a number of excellent ideas from Land Rover club members whose ingenuity at the usage of limited space far exceeded my own. Hidden compartments under the seats and in the door frames. A nifty place for melamine plates and cutlery in the back door. Complete with a fold-down cover that doubled cleverly as a work space for the preparation of basic meals. Small cupboards along the sides of the load bed, with a pull-out bunk should I decide to sleep inside the vehicle rather than in the roof-top tent. All the while, week-end excursions with the Land Rover club had greatly increased my off-road driving ability. Most importantly, I could cautiously contribute to discussions on the merits of the Salisbury diff. I was almost ready to set off on The Grand Safari.

* * *

Late one Friday afternoon, about four months after I had first reported for duty at the garage, Fred and I, with a little help from Trevor, made a major dent in a bottle of good 10 year old Cape brandy. In a wide-ranging conversation we talked about the bush, 4 x 4 vehicles and rugby. We sniggered contemptuously at those who had never ground crankshafts or taken off heads.

Outside stood my completely rebuilt Land Rover. I had decided against festooning the vehicle with shovels and high lift jacks and powerful spotlights. And I felt there was no need for wide wheels. The only visible accessory was the fold away roof top tent and game-viewing platform with its ladder. On arrival at a camp site, I would be able to erect the tent in three minutes. Two minutes later I would be sitting on my folding chair, glass of chilled wine in hand, awaiting the arrival of the first lions.

I bade Fred a fond farewell; handed over a cut glass decanter for his brandy. The scowl didn't leave his face, but I thought I detected a glistening in his eyes. I sincerely hoped that Trevor would never ever be in a position where he had to let Fred go.

It was now mid-year. Winter in southern Africa. The right time to visit the bushveld. The odyssey was about to begin.

I was about to answer the call of the Wilderness.

4

I called Anton and suggested that we meet for a glass of wine at the old watering hole. The renovation of my vehicle was complete, I revealed casually, and it would be good to share a glass or three before I set off.

For the wildness.

I had been lucky enough to find a parking space right outside the pub and my ancient Land Rover stood, splendidly incongruous, among the yuppie cars with their mag wheels, rear end spoilers and leather seats. Already I was beginning to feel a certain disdain for dissolute city life.

"This is really well done", said Anton, a hint of what I thought was disbelief in his voice as he gazed admiringly at the reborn Land Rover. I smiled modestly. Shrugged in an off-hand - nothing really - way.

"Who did it for you?" he asked.

"I did it myself", I replied a little peevishly, hoping that Fred would forgive my omitting mention of his considerable technical input. Anton said nothing but he raised his eyebrows and nodded approvingly.

We were well into our first bottle of wine when Anton casually mentioned that his sister would be joining us. She had set off, many years ago, for England, he explained, to study physiotherapy and after qualifying she had started a new life in London, eventually opening her own practice. She had just returned to South Africa to see her family and to take a brief break from her busy career.

Little did I know that events were about to take a totally unexpected turn.

* * *

It was a case of the old cliché about conversation stopping when a particularly beautiful woman walked into a bar. Jessica put her arm around Anton's shoulders and gave him a sisterly peck on the cheek.

"Jess, this is Denis," as I rose clumsily to my feet, sending my bar stool clattering to the floor. Before I could mumble something horribly predictable about how amazing it was that someone as ugly as Anton could have such a lovely sister, he told Jessica that Denis was about to set off on a trans-Africa safari in an old Land Rover. Not to the casinos and topless beaches, he added earnestly – but off the beaten track to the Real Africa. Anton tried hard to sound sincere but I thought I detected a slightly mocking tone in his intro-duction.

"Sounds great," said Jessica. "Can I come with you?" she asked in that very British accent that is so admired in many parts of the world. Her smile was amused rather than impressed. I did my best to look calm and masterful – just like someone who was more than capable of handling such an adventure - as I stared into twinkling dark brown eyes and shook her hand.

A couple of hours later I was feeling nothing but goodwill towards all men and women. I was on my way!! Both Anton and I had spent a bit of time in the bush and I guess our tales of encounters with hostile beasts were growing more extravagant by the minute as the evening went by. Anton had been charged by an angry buffalo; he had awoken one morning to find he was sharing his sleeping bag with a cobra. Close encounters with enormous lions and enraged elephants were commonplace. We raised several glasses to Africa and its magnificent wildlife – agreed that we had lost touch with our glorious heritage. How great it was that I would be setting off to-morrow to right that wrong.

All the while, Jessica - effortlessly matching us glass for glass - listened politely, having confessed early in the evening that, much to her regret, she had not spent any time at all getting to know the animals in her country of birth.

"Too busy massaging people and running triathlons" Anton declared, laughing rather too loudly. "You're a triathlon man aren't you Denis?" poking his finger into my ribs. "What's your best time for a triathlon?" he demanded. I was about to give a modest cough and reveal that while I had never been able to spend as much time as I would have liked on training, I did have a couple of podium finishes in my age group, when Anton mentioned that his sister had been part of the England triathlon team. Jessica looked at me expectantly, an interested, friendly sort of smile on her face.

"I don't recall," frowning and shaking my head in a forgetful way.

It was an appropriate time for me to withdraw. For I, Denis Shirley, was departing early to-morrow morning to go home to what little was left of the Garden of Eden.

I gave Anton a hug and turned to his gorgeous sister. "Lovely to meet you" – I couldn't think of anything clever to say to Jessica. "And I hope you will find a bit of time to see something of the wildlife while you're here". After all our stories, how could she not?

"I hope so too."

"Then why don't you go with Denis? He should see something – when he sobers up". Anton seemed quite pleased with his own joke.

Jessica smiled tolerantly at her brother. "Good idea. Anything to get away from you. What time are you leaving to-morrow"? she asked politely, looking into my eyes.

"Around 5.30 I think".

I climbed into my Land Rover. A moment's panic when the key wouldn't turn. Relief as I remembered that the starter button lurked below the dashboard. I should know by now! A brief wave to Anton and Jessica and I was on my way.

* * *

Early the next morning, brother and sister arrived at the gate of my townhouse just as I reversed the Land Rover out of my garage.

"Perfectly timed" said Anton, opening the back door of the vehicle and depositing Jessica's carry-all into the Landie. He looked up at the roof, then into the back. "Who's going to sleep on top?" he asked as he closed the door, evidently pleased with his double entendre.

Jess climbed into the passenger seat and gave me a wide smile.

"Let's go" she said.

Speechless, I engaged first gear and set off for the N1.

5

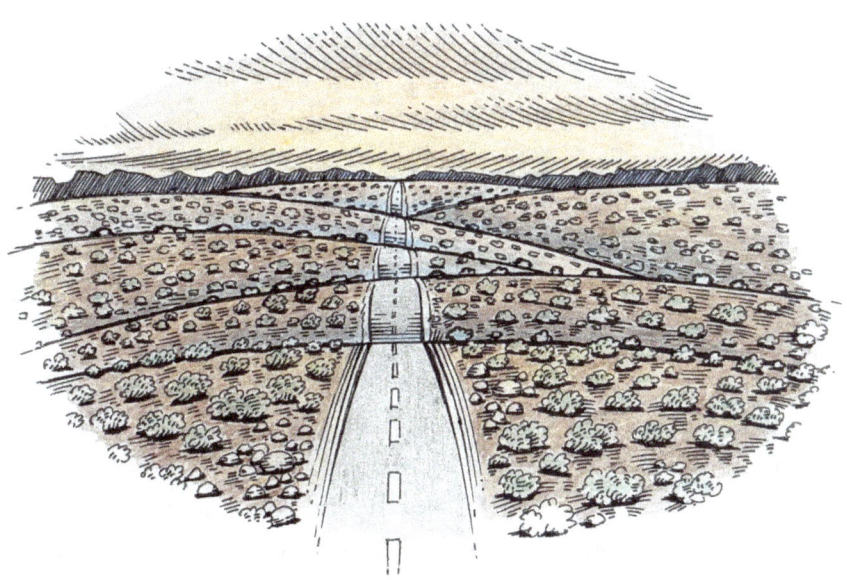

I had lived all my life in Africa and the magic of the Dark Continent flowed richly in my veins. Africa is the cradle of mankind and you can never truly leave her, I had been told by friends who had gone elsewhere to seek their fortunes. It will always be in your blood, they said. So perhaps my unplanned early retirement had indeed been a blessing in disguise, leading to a sort of atavistic homecoming for a jaded marketing executive. A path to a new world in which stock problems and board room jealousies were irrelevant – even faintly ludicrous. And if time was running out for the Real Africa what better time than now?

My ponderings were disturbed by a movement on my left. Soon after we left Cape Town Jess had drawn her legs up, wrapped her arms around her knees and fallen asleep. Giving me the opportunity to sneak quick, furtive glances at her. I eventually decided she was about as beautiful as any woman could be. Classic, high cheekbones. A full, sensuous mouth. And those beautiful brown eyes. Now peacefully closed.

I couldn't quite understand how it had happened that she was now in the passenger seat of my elderly Land Rover, accompanying me on a trip into the wilds of Africa. I had never contemplated having company and while the Land Rover, essentially, offered two separate "bedrooms" there was the matter of washing and dressing and such things. I supposed that if, at any stage, Jess wanted to abandon the odyssey, it would be possible to find some way of getting her back to Cape Town. Not much I could do at this stage.

She stirred, opened her eyes and stretched out her legs just as the sun appeared over the Hex River Mountains. We were ambling up the N1 making our way through the craggy splendour of the mountains that guard the Cape winelands from the rest of South Africa. What lay ahead was possibly the longest stretch of straight road in the continent, leading ever onwards through the Klein Karoo. The "Land of Thirst" with its scant vegetation and weirdly shaped rocks and hills. An area to be left behind as quickly as possible by those focused on sales targets and production schedules. But those who have been released from such burdens are able to delight in the crystal-clear air and brilliant star lit nights and gaze in wonder at the spectacular sunrise that heralds a new day in the Karoo. I wondered if there was anything similar within easy reach of Jessica's London.

She didn't say anything but there was a small smile on her face as she watched the sun slowly rise.

"Did you know that you snore?" I asked.

"I do not!"

"Yes you do. It's not at all an offensive sort of snore. It's more the gentle, contemplative type. Thoughtful, one might say."

No reply.

"We're in the Karoo now" I informed Jess.

This part of South Africa has a fascinating geography and I was keen to share what little I could remember of it from my distant school days with a visitor from England. Hoping my memory would not fail me too badly.

"The Karoo has one of the richest collections of pre-historic fossils in the world – some of them 250 million years old", I revealed.

I started to lecture now – after all, Jess had not spent nearly as much time in this part of the world as her brother and I and she would probably know little if anything about the Karoo.

"There are traces of glacial activity which indicate that millions of years ago, this part of South Africa was covered by ice", I explained in a learned way. "But then a profound and rapid climatic change saw the ice retreat and in its place came this huge swampy basin," sweeping my left hand majestically across the dashboard, "filled with primitive plants and dinosaurs and other mysterious amphibious creatures whose names I forget".

"Pareiasaurus and Titanosuchids" Jessica revealed dreamily in that very British accent.

What?!

I was learning. As with the subject of the triathlons, I decided not to continue with the lecture.

Jess arched her back in a feline sort of way and tapped the cubby hole between the seats. "What's in here?" she asked. "Am I allowed to take a look?"

Having suffered many thousands of uncomfortable kilometres on the rather primitive three seats found in the older Land Rovers of my army days, I had fitted two comfortable single seats and between them a handy compartment in which to put useful things and a few of my favourite CDs. A good quality sound system was one of the few luxuries I had allowed myself.

She flicked through my carefully compiled selection.

"Shuman's Carnaval. Hhmmm. I don't much care for Schuman but I find this piece very uplifting".

Dvorak cello concerto – and Jacqueline du Pre". An approving nod.

I felt quite pleased with myself. So far so good.

"Brahms – The Symphonies." Another tick. Things were looking even better. "Mozart's requiem – oh dear".

"In sad memory of all the animals shot by Great White Hunters," seemed like a good response.

"Elgar's Nimrod. Such a dignified piece."

"In memory of the British Empire," I replied – now even more pleased with myself.

And then. "Springbok…Hits…Volume 3?" Mock surprise - a wide, innocent smile.

Ah yes. I have nothing against the Springbok Hits. Nothing at all. But with CD space at a premium, they would not have made the cut. I remembered going to bid farewell to Trevor and Fred a couple of days before I left Cape Town. Fred had given the Land Rover one last look-over and had peeked into my CD box. His frown had grown deeper as he went through my careful selection. "Funeral music" was his disapproving verdict. He disappeared into his workshop – emerged a minute later with his Springbok Hits Volume 3 CD. I thanked him profusely and slipped the CD into the compartment. And forgot about it.

* * *

"Where are we going, by the way?" Jessica asked.

Bit late to ask now, isn't it?

"To the Okavango", I replied, raising my voice above the thudding music. She had inserted Springbok Hits Volume 3 into the CD player and turned up the volume.

Where I had been hoping for a little peace and quiet, I almost added.

It had never been my intention to work to a carefully planned itinerary. Rather I had wanted to go where fancy took me – starting in the Okavango Delta in Botswana, making my way up through Savuti, into the Chobe area and the Zambezi River. I could then head west into Namibia or east into Zimbabwe – or maybe even further north to Tanzania and Kenya. I would have all the time in the world to make up my mind. Without having to consider where someone else might fancy going.

I explained the plan – possibly a little peevishly.

"Great!!" said Jess enthusiastically. "Super". I waited for an alternative (probably more intelligent) plan but none came.

6

The dignified pace of a senior Land Rover is very much at odds with the urgent haste of the monster trucks that thunder up and down South Africa's main highway. Many whose zombie-like drivers seemed to have a primeval need to nestle as close as possible to the rear end of slower moving vehicles before overtaking in a cloud of diesel fumes and a roar of disapproval.

So it was a relief to reach the refreshment point and filling station at Three Sisters and turn off the N1 highway to head north on the road less travelled to the Botswana border.

We were now in Kalahari country. Though very dry – parts of the area are sometimes without rain for several years – there is a rugged beauty in the hardy vegetation and distant mountains. And those travelling below the speed of sound are rewarded by frequent sightings of small antelope and a rich variety of bird life.

It had been raining steadily when we had left but now that the Cape mountains were well behind us and we were heading into the hinterland, the skies were a wintry pale blue with just a few brush-strokes of white cloud on the horizon. No malodorous pollution here; no smudge of industrial smog in this part of the world.

The Magic of the Journey was by now fully upon me. Gazing out over the Land Rover's bonnet, listening to the engine turning over quietly and comfortably, keeping an eye on the countryside steadily swirling past, made my spirits soar. The wilderness lay ahead – I was now on my way Home. I imagined Mr. Baldwin back in his large, beautifully redecorated office in Cape Town – perhaps even now he was setting free another luckless soul from my marketing department. I felt sympathy, even tenderness, for Baldwin. Bless him – and his merger. And let us not forget his Personal Assistant.

Though she said nothing, I had the feeling that Jess was sharing my feelings of contentment. While I had not expected to have any company on my odyssey, I had by now come to terms with the consequences of the off-hand invitation her brother had made on my behalf. The Landie could accommodate two people – I could take the roof-top tent and Jess could sleep in the back of the vehicle. I knew nothing of Jess and her life in London and while I guessed that Anton would have told her a little of my background – my recent divorce, my daughter, my being made redundant, the fact that I was not involved in any sort of romantic relationship - she knew very little about me. Yet here we were, a man and a woman, setting off into the wilds in a Land Rover. I decided that it would be better not to complicate things and to push notions of any sort of romance out of my mind. Best to regard Jessica as a very pleasant (and very good-looking) travelling companion. And perhaps it was better to have a partner when travelling way off the beaten track, I reasoned. Perhaps we might end up broken down in some remote corner of the delta and I would discover that Jess was as familiar with Land Rover engines as she was with triathlons and the prehistoric creatures of the Karoo.

I had planned the first overnight stop at Kimberley. Always willing to share the exciting story of the Kimberley diamond rush, I told Jess how in 1866 (as the story goes) a farmer noticed what looked like a large shiny stone in the hands of a neighbour's child and offered to have the magistrate at the tiny settlement of Colesberg take a look at the stone. The magistrate, it seemed, knew a bit about these things because he used the stone to carve his initials on a pane of glass. The 21.25 carat diamond was subsequently sold to the Governor of the Cape for the vast sum of £500. This launched one of the greatest diamond rushes of all time. By 1870 ten thousand eager prospectors and hangers-on were camped on the banks of the Vaal River and when even richer pickings were discovered on a farm purchased – for £50 - by the brothers de Beer, Diamond City was born. Within months the prospectors and the camp followers swarmed into the area and it wasn't long before the bars and the dance halls, the madams and the boxing rings were doing a roaring trade. Frantically digging away with their picks and shovels the fortune seekers soon created the largest man-made hole in the world – 400 metres deep and 500 metres wide.

The de Beer brothers, undoubtedly after a great deal of very careful thought, sold their farm for £6000 thereby surrendering a major share of the tens of millions of pounds worth of gems that the property was to eventually yield.

The Mother of All Diamonds, of course, was the Star of Africa. Weighing in at a hefty 3,106 carats, it was unearthed in 1905 at the Cullinan mine. It produced several stones of various sizes – the largest of which was eventually presented to King Edward VII. It now resides in the Sovereign's Sceptre with Cross.

The First World War brought an end to mining at Kimberley's Big Hole. The bars closed down, those madams who had not moved on to the even more promising opportunities at the goldfields to the north went on their way and the town was never the same again.

I hoped that my account of this interesting chapter of South Africa's history was more or less accurate. And wondered if Jess might correct me on the details of the Star of Africa.

"I wonder if there might be a couple more Cullinans lying around somewhere near here?" she mused.

"Might be. But I fear you are more than a hundred years too late."

* * *

We pulled into the camp site at Kimberley and parked the Land Rover in a quiet corner. As I opened a bottle of nicely chilled Chardonnay, Jess laid down a thin mat on the grass and proceeded to contort her lithe body into seemingly impossible positions eventually ending up standing perfectly still on her head for several minutes.

Something for the animals in the Okavango to look forward to I thought.

When refrigerated storage space is at a premium, one has to shop along the way, so there was not a large choice on the menu for the first night – especially as I had catered for one not two. But Jess had brought her own supplies and in the days to come she somehow managed, in a very subtle way, to assume super-competent control of the catering. All the while ensuring that the wine perfectly complemented the food.

It had been a long day on the road, with another few to follow, so I could hear bed calling.

Remembering Anton's attempt at a clever joke just before we left, I suggested that I sleep in the roof top tent while Jess took the Land Rover's bunk bed.

"If you think you can manage the ladder" she said sweetly as she climbed into the back of the vehicle and closed the door firmly behind her.

7

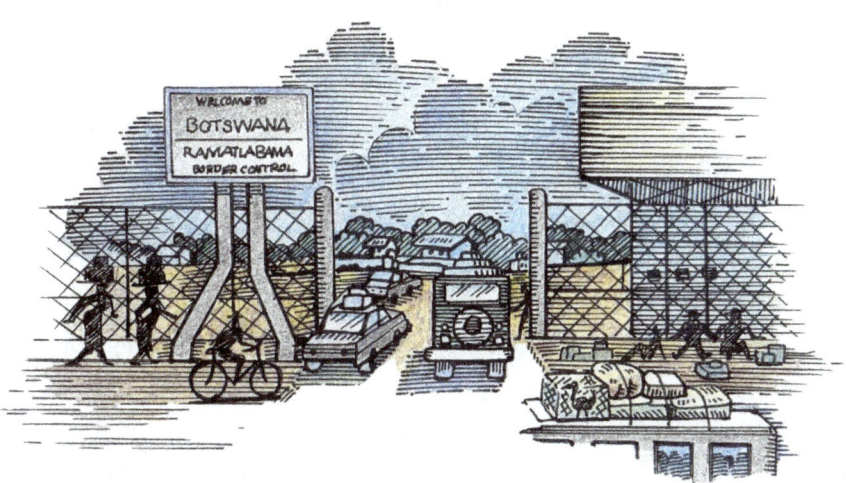

D awn found us on the road again and it wasn't long before we turned off the N 12 at Warrenton and took the R49 for Mafikeng – the "Place of Rocks".

Hoping that my lectures on the history of South Africa would be at least moderately entertaining I launched into an account of the famous siege of Mafikeng. As best I could remember the story. During the Anglo Boer War, I recounted to Jess, the small town, under the command of the redoubtable Colonel Robert Baden-Powell, had been half-heartedly besieged by the Boers. Determined to hold out at all costs, the Colonel had set about constructing an elaborate and, to the townsfolk, probably bewildering network of breastworks, trenches and bunkers. In the absence of a really deter-mined effort by the Boers the Colonel and his charges were able to defend the fortress for seven long months. This heroic defence caught the imagination of the English public and when the siege was eventually lifted by British troops, celebrations in London reached almost hysterical proportions. It was as though a great victory had been won.

"Always be prepared. The Boy Scouts would have been proud of you sir." Jess nodded approvingly.

At Mafikeng we turned on to the A1 to the border post at Ramatlabama.

Border posts in Africa have a character all of their own. A cast which will include two or three ancient buses, their flanks covered by the dust and mud of never ending journeys across the Dark Continent. Roof racks laden with battered suitcases, securely trussed cardboard boxes, old bicycles, perhaps a caged chicken or two. Here and there on the ground ominous oil stains bearing testimony to valiant engines that had eventually succumbed to countless kilometres along the unforgiving arteries of Africa. A large number of people hanging about the buildings – men, women and children – with no apparent hope of ever moving on.

Some sound asleep under the trees, with that amazing ability that African people have to sleep peacefully on the ground with nothing more than an elbow or a forearm for a pillow. The ambiance is one of infinite patience, a quality noticeably absent from the environment I had recently vacated but one central to people from rural Africa. A philosophy in which urgency has no place; rather, there rules the quiet conviction that – ultimately - there will be an answer.

I parked the Land Rover next to a battered 1970s Peugeot 404, a vehicle prized in Africa for its legendary durability. The bonnet wired shut, well faded grey paintwork subtly complemented by one hand painted blue door. Tyres as smooth as the proverbial baby's bum.

We entered the Customs building and joined the queue. Five months out of the world of commerce and I was beginning to understand that life without deadlines was a real possibility. That time – under certain circumstances – was not money. So I resolved to allow the atmosphere of restful somnolence to overcome me as we took our places behind a large woman with a baby slumbering peacefully in a cotton shawl tied onto her back. In one corner, a small girl effortlessly hitting high C after high C as she stamped repeatedly on a by now well flattened cool drink can.

Above the counter, a large full colour photograph of the President of Botswana gazed down imperiously at the travellers.

Before the customs official a man in a faded blue jersey with large holes in the elbows slumped hopelessly on the counter, one hand shielding his eyes from the accusing stare of the President. There were, it seemed, major complications with his travel documents – a speedy resolution of the problem seemed unlikely. I wondered how Jess – just a few days out from a very different life in England, would handle the situation – but she appeared to be perfectly relaxed and at peace.

"Much the same as Heathrow," she murmured.

In the fullness of time we emerged from the Customs buildings and rolled into Botswana.

The country has an interesting history and I felt I should share it with my travelling companion.

More than 10,000 years ago, I lectured, the San people, lived their nomadic existence with the animals but the last few hundred years had seen black and white races advancing into the country – an intrusion that was to result in the gradual disappearance of the San and their hunter/gatherer lifestyle. Then came the time - in the age of the British Empire – for what was to be called the Bechuana-land Protectorate. HMG having deemed that this part of the conti-nent (and any useful resources it might happen to have), should fall under the protection of the Empire.

In later years, as the Empire steadily declined and then completely disintegrated, it was on to an independent Botswana.

Bigger in area than France, Botswana was for many years in the embarrassing position of being listed as one of the world's 25 poorest countries. It was later found to have great mineral wealth – copper, nickel, coal, iron ore and - at a place called Orapa - diamonds. This wealth rapidly propelled the country out of the Poorest Nations Club though mining activities inevitably created areas of friction with the wild life.

Jess listened politely to the lesson.

* * *

We were soon on the road to Gaborone, Botswana's main city. On past Mahalapye and Palapye, then to an overnight stop at Francis-town – the site of Africa's first gold rush.

Records show that in 1866, one of the many hunters in the area shot an elephant that fortuitously died at the site of what turned out to be a long forgotten mine. Later, more ancient workings were found along the Tati River and a flood of prospectors and traders from all around the world sped hopefully into the area. In the old workings were found traces of a vanished people – possibly the same culture that built the mysterious kingdom of Zimbabwe. The gold fever – mild in comparison with that in the Witwatersrand - had all but run its course by the mid-1870s.

One more day on the road and we would be at Maun, the last town before the delta, where we would stock up with provisions and water – and fill the specially made long-range tanks.

The road to Maun took Jess and me past the Makgadikgadi Salt Pans and game reserve, 6,500 square kilometres of flat, glaring white sand, where once had lived an astonishing number and variety of animals. The lure of furs, skins, feathers and ivory brought the hunters and the traders hurrying out to the area and there followed, in the late eighteenth century, the most appalling butchery of countless thousands of lions, leopards and elephants, not to mention ostriches, smaller game and meat animals. A frenzy of killing that was hindered only by the remoteness of the pans and the impenetrable nature of certain parts of the area.

Mozart's Requiem seemed like a good choice for background music.

The descendants of the survivors of the massacre now roam the labyrinthine wilderness of salt pans and burnished grasslands, waiting patiently for the infrequent and violent thunderstorms that briefly fill the pans to a depth of a few millimetres. Then, an infinite number of pink flamingos and pelicans gather in the shallow lake as though to pay their respects to the victims of man's greed and short-sightedness. The animals lead a nomadic existence in the Makgadikgadi, following the sparse rains to the north and after observing a few moments silence, they return south to the Boteti River for the dry winter months.

We pulled into Maun in mid-afternoon. With two mouths to feed for an unknown number of weeks and one small fridge, careful thought had to be given to the list of provisions. It is not possible in the Okavango to pop down to the corner store for some forgotten item.

With dusk falling and satisfied with our purchases we made our way to the camping area just outside Maun. Next stop – the Okavango.

8

The enormity of this corner of Africa is difficult to grasp. Fifteen thousand square kilometres of largely uninhabited wilderness. Many people will spend a lifetime never more than a few metres from the next person but in the weeks to come, there would be times when Jessica and I could be up to fifty kilometres from the nearest human being. A thought that might be disconcerting for those who find comfort in the constant presence of their fellowmen and women but one which I – and, it seemed, Jess - relished.

We bade farewell to our fellow travellers in the camping site at Maun and having made sure that the Landie was fully prepared for the challenge that lay ahead, set off for the Okavango. It wasn't too long before we reached the end of the tar road and moved onto gravel. And then came the sand and it was time to engage four-wheel drive – and an opportunity for me to demonstrate my recently acquired off-road driving skills to my beautiful travel mate. I hoped I would not be found wanting. From now on we would be swirling cautiously through treacherous sand that could very quickly trap an unwary driver and bring down upon him the humiliation of having to shovel a way out.

Welcome to the delta.

* * *

The Okavango River starts life as a number of humble trickles of summer rain in the mountains of Angola, about three hundred kilometres from the Atlantic Ocean. Slowly but surely these trickles grow into highland streams which eventually meet up to form the Okavango River. Flowing strong and deep the river sets out across the broad face of the subcontinent until it comes up against the mighty Kalahari Desert. It then splits into a bewildering multitude of rivers, swamps, lakes and forests, so numerous as to be beyond count. A captivating but crazy maze of palm covered islands with channels that will flow this way in one year, that way in another, thereby creating one of the world's last great wildernesses. And an impossible challenge for cartographers.

We entered this African wonderland through the Moremi wildlife reserve. Named after Chief Moremi 111 of the Tawana people the area is home to possibly the greatest concentration of wild animals and bird species in Africa – and possibly - the world. From here on, we were about as close to the original Garden of Eden as it is possible to be.

Having paid the entrance fees, we were soon winding our way happily through the grasslands and mopani trees but as it was by now mid-morning we didn't expect to see much game. Africa's wildlife is more active at night than in the day, mostly resting during the heat and feeding or hunting during the cool of the night. So with the sun overhead, we parked under an enormous sausage tree on the banks of a lagoon to follow the sensible custom of the locals.

Though at first glance we had the lagoon to ourselves, a few moments at its side soon revealed that this was not so. A large, saddle-billed stork stood motionless on the other side of the lagoon, apparently deep in thought. A heron picked its way gravely through the shallows, peering intently into the water. From atop a dead tree trunk, a fish eagle rent the sky with its yearning, soulful cry. And a solitary roan antelope stood motionless under a huge camelthorn tree on the opposite side of the lagoon.

The leaves rustled gently as a caressing breeze took the heat out of the winter sun. Peace, perfect peace. Henry – or was his name Harry? - Baldwin was beginning to take on almost mystical characteristics; things like five-year budgets were becoming the stuff of unpleasant, surrealistic dreams. And what was Henry's PA's name?

Jess went to the water's edge to rinse her plate. Sitting comfortably on my fold-up chair I focused idly on an object floating in the water some thirty meters from the bank. A piece of driftwood? A water plant? Or what might be the head of a very large crocodile? The delta is prime real estate for the African representatives of the crocodilian species and it was well worthwhile to remember this fact when close to water. I would not want to have to explain to Anton that his lovely sister had been taken by a crocodile.

While I was sure that Jess knew enough about crocodiles to be prudent at the water's edge, I felt I needed to remind her of the creature's terrifying hunting technique. How, almost totally submerged, it would drift slowly closer to its prey, only the eyes, ears and the tip of its nostrils showing in the water. Then, when it reckoned that the distance was right, it would submerge completely and switch to attack mode.

Trying not to sound too dramatic, I concluded the first part of the lecture with a graphic description of how, in the final moments prior to the attack, fore and hind legs would be tucked into the great body; the muscular, immensely powerful tail would thrust the hunter forward like a deadly torpedo. Then there would be an explosive lunge and the fearsome jaws would snap shut in a vice-like grip from which there was seldom any hope of escape.

I paused for a moment's solemn reflection.

Then, warming to my theme, I continued with the lecture.

While these jaws are highly effective at crushing things, crocodiles can't chew so they are obliged to swallow their meals whole. This does not present a problem with small prey but even for a crocodile, swallowing something like a large antelope in one gulp is not possible. A different technique is required.

Jessica was listening patiently and I felt that she should not be spared any details.

So, the talk continued, the crocodile drags large prey under the water and spins around rapidly, cleverly twisting off limbs and large pieces of flesh. It then seizes one of these pieces in its mouth, returns to the surface and jubilantly throws its head back to swallow. After snatching a few quick breaths, it eagerly returns underwater for the next course. Not what would be considered good manners in high society, but it works for the crocodiles, I concluded.

Jess digested this information for a few moments. Then asked – "Why do crocodiles lie on sand banks with their mouths open"?

"Good question. I believe they do this to cool themselves. And to show off their fearful teeth".

"Like that one over there"? asked Jess, pointing to a huge croc lying uncomfortably close to where I was sitting. A reminder that when in the bush, one should always keep one eye on your left, one eye on your right, one eye in front of you and one eye behind you. As casually as I could I moved my chair to a safer position. There to continue the lecture – and to show that there is another side to crocs - one with which I hoped Jess would more easily identify.

I told her that the devotion of crocodile mothers is legendary. When the time has come to lay her eggs, the mother will carefully search for the right location for her nest. It must meet a number of criteria. It must be close to the river, clean, not too hot and in close enough proximity to her own resting place. To prepare the nest she supports herself with her tail, then laboriously digs – with short back legs not ideally suited to such a task – a large sandy hole. In it she will lay up to 150 eggs which she then – again with her short back legs – covers with sand and diligently guards, never straying far from the site, despite hunger and heat. The eggs – much prized delicacies - have to be protected from merciless thieving by a variety of skilful burglars. Lizards, baboons and hyenas will plunder the nests despite the mother's vigilance.

"What part does the crocodile father play in the making of the nest? And in the protection of the young"? Jess asked in a matter of fact way.

I had to admit that the father was a bit neglectful in these areas and would probably be chilling with a couple of mates at their favourite watering hole during these times. I thought it better to continue as swiftly as possible.

Prior to hatching, I explained, the baby crocodiles begin to vocalise, bringing the good news of their impending birth to their nearby mother. Who rushes up in great excitement and eagerly scrapes aside the sand to welcome her new born into a dangerous and hostile world. She then either proudly escorts the hatchlings to the water or carries the little fellows down to the river in her great mouth. Jaws that can clamp shut with horrifying pressure can also roll a vocalising egg gently enough to crack it and facilitate the exit of a tiny hatchling. It's a desperate race to the relative safety of the water. Storks and fish eagles welcome the babies by eating them and there is nothing that the mother can do to stop the pillaging. Probably no more than 5% of new-born crocodiles ever make it to adulthood and those that do not fall prey while eggs or hatchlings, still have to survive a couple of dangerous years before they can start to relax a little. And then they can exact revenge on the water birds and other predators that murdered their brothers and sisters.

These facts called for a look at the bigger picture for crocodiles.

I explained that despite this high infant mortality, crocodiles have a remarkable record of survival - their size and strength ensured that they generally came out on top in the struggle for survival. In their time on Mother Earth, they have escaped the great extinctions and ice ages that saw the demise of the likes of the dinosaur – and of a number of man's early ancestors.

All that changed, of course, when crocodile skin shoes and handbags became must have items in fashionable wardrobes. Then, the crocodile species, which had been around for 200 million years or so, was brought to the verge of extinction within the space of little more than half a century. Another name to be added to the list of threatened species.

I paused to give Jess the opportunity to confess that she had, at some time or other, owned something made from the skin of a crocodile but she said nothing.

She did, however, mention as we walked back to the Land Rover that she had not wanted to interrupt the fascinating lesson on crocodiles to bring to my attention the fact that a large puff adder had made its way slowly past my chair while I was lecturing.

* * *

We set off eventually for our first night's stop in Moremi – Third Bridge campsite. Facilities were not entirely what one might have hoped for given the steep entrance fees – comprising no more than cleared spaces beneath the fig and sausage trees.

"Where are the toilets"? Jess asked as I parked the Landie under a friendly tree.

"Over there" I replied, pointing to a couple of large overgrown mounds.

Jess looked a little confused.

"Behind those mounds?" she asked.

"No" I replied. "Those are the toilets. Or they were until the elephants knocked them down. I guess the reserve officials would have figured,

quite reasonably, that it would not be worthwhile repairing the damage - the elephants would only trample the toilets again. And grass and creepers would soon hide the remnants".

"So… ahh….?

"There's a shovel strapped under the rear end of the Landie," I called.

"And remember not to stray too far from the vehicle. Third Bridge is not a good place to be caught with your pants down. As the saying goes".

An obvious, rather corny comment I know.

"Showers? Baths?"

"Resting at peace with the toilets".

I pointed to the small stream that flowed through the camping area.

No hot water but as pure and clean as anything in a five star hotel and it was an indescribable luxury for us to slip off the crude wooden bridge into the cold depths of the stream, reasonably assured that there were no crocodiles in attendance. All the while I did my best not to notice that Jess had a body that would have made her the number one choice for a company advertising swimsuits in a sports magazine.

* * *

Not fifty meters from the campsite, we noticed, there had been what was almost certainly a lion kill. Several large vultures flapped awkwardly around the remains of a kudu bull, lurching threateningly towards small jackal, eager to share in the spoils. Not far off, two hyenas were going to work on large bones, their all-powerful jaws performing the crushing business without any difficulty. Hyenas have the strongest jaws in the animal kingdom.

We speculated that the kill would have taken place in the early hours of the morning. We imagined the lionesses watching the herd for several minutes. Perhaps there would have been cubs in the background, doing their best to contain their excitement as they watched their mothers going about their deadly task. They might have worked as a team - there have been instances where lionesses display remarkably well co-ordinated teamwork during a hunt. Or they might have worked independently and one of them had been lucky enough to bring down the unfortunate antelope. Lions are not terribly efficient hunters and their success rate is nothing to be proud of. As they spend around 22 hours of each day relaxing or sleeping soundly, their fitness levels are not the highest in the animal kingdom. So if they do not strike it lucky with their first lethal charge, the stamina to pursue their prey is often sadly lacking. Leaving them panting heavily and bitterly disappointed.

Quite apart from which, a lioness has to exercise a certain discretion when hunting - a jaw broken by a kick from a giraffe or a buffalo amounts to a slow and painful death sentence. So even the Queen of the Beasts has many challenges to face, many dangers to avoid. But last night, evidently, luck had been with them and the pride would have feasted well. While the scavengers waited in an agony of impatience to fight for the scraps.

While a pride's territory might be huge, anything upwards from thirty five square kilometres, we knew that the lions would probably not be far away. The males would have eaten well enough just a few hours ago to make travel of any distance unattractive – and there was every chance that the pride, or one or two members - might return to the kill to-night. Then there would be fierce competition with the hyenas. Who – contrary to their unfortunate and undeserved reputation as rather cowardly, skulking scavengers – would be no pushover for a lioness or two. Especially if the hyena matriarch was able to summon support from her clan and orchestrate the famous hyena battle plan.

Hyenas are experts at creating chaos, dancing in for a nip here, darting in for a bite there. All the time circling the battleground while maintaining a demented cacophony of yelps and whoops, cackles and barks – enough to drive any lioness to distraction. Their teamwork is superb and unless a lioness concentrates on one individual, she will find herself sidetracked and distracted and totally outwitted by the clan. Which could well lead her to retire in disgust. So the evening held the promise of first class entertainment.

With that in mind, we decided to have an early supper and then position the Land Rover on the edge of the clearing about 20 meters from where the kill had taken place. This would put us in the best seats in the house but as we were the only people in the camp-site, there was no need to queue or arrive early.

By the time the sun had gone down and dusk was turning to night, we had finished our meal and, a slightly chilled, full-bodied Cabernet freshly uncorked, taken our places in the Land Rover.

Let the show begin.

9

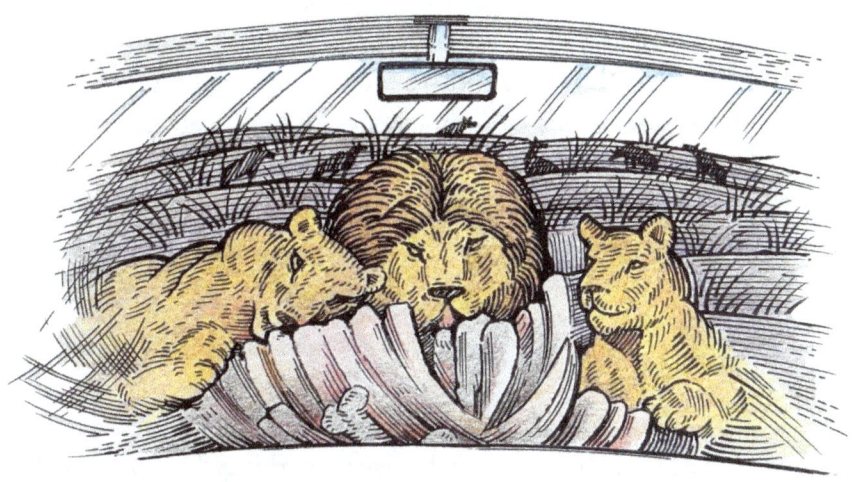

I had by now become very fond of Jess and I was really enjoying her company. I had told her a little of my life – my work in the company, a couple of tales about Anton and me, my divorce and the sorrow of trying to convince my beautiful daughter that a good divorce was going to be better than a bad marriage. I knew that Anton and Jessica's parents had divorced when she was very young but not that she and her mom had left South Africa to start a new life in England. She had completed school there, then gone on to study for her degree. She had been asked to try out for England's triathlon squad but a knee injury had put paid to any hopes of making the team. By the time she had recovered, she was too busy in her physiotherapy practise to devote enough time to training. So we were – at a very leisurely pace – talking things over and getting to know each other.

Most importantly, we found we were able to gently tease each other with no risk of any resentment. Jess had a lively, mischievous sense of humour and a kind, caring personality that one couldn't help but love. I still could not believe that Anton's off-hand invitation to Jess to join me on my odyssey/idiocy would turn out so wonderfully.

Keeping an eye on the hyenas who were working diligently on the carcass, we had sipped our way through the better part of the Cabernet when we heard the lions.

There is something awe-inspiring about the roar of a lion. Especially when it is working in concert with a number of fellow lions. Lions do not simply roar haphazardly; there are certain procedures to be followed when roaring; certain guidelines to be adhered to.

The concert usually begins with a low groan, presumably from the most important lion in the pride. After due consideration the first groan is followed by a second and then a third – possibly some sort of tuning exercise to make sure that all the lions are in the same key. After a few moments suspense, and the lions having decided that all is in order, the principal lion's roar rolls across the silent night. A brief pause to consider the quality of this roar and the second lion responds with a roar of its own. Then a third and then a fourth. We had no idea how far away the lions were. Possibly a couple of kilometres – the roar of a lion can be heard up to eight kilometres away. But it seemed that the Land Rover, and the very ground on which it stood, vibrated and trembled at the power of the sound.

Without knowing it, I suspect, Jess had taken a very firm grip on my left wrist.

As suddenly as it had begun, the roaring ceased. After a few minutes, it was followed by a series of coughs and grunts and a hiss or two – presumably a prelude to the second movement. Which, when it came, indicated that the lions were steadily drawing nearer.

This realisation brought about a feeling of extraordinary humility to the occupants of the Land Rover. The thought that we were all alone in the bush with an unknown number of 220 kilo-gram lions padding purposefully towards us had, I felt sure, the same effect on us as it must have had on our primitive ancestors. This was a time to reflect on past indiscretions and unkind acts and to ask for forgiveness for all trespasses. I realised that in all the years I had worked against Henry, Harry (or was it Charles?) Baldwin, I had not once sent him a Christmas card. Perhaps it was now too late to atone for this oversight.

Would retreat be possible? Surely even a pride of lions couldn't pull down a fully grown Land Rover?

The hyenas, it was clear, shared our unease. None of them were chewing now and only one was still lying down. The approaching lions had the full, undivided attention of all present.

I poured another glass of Cab for Jessica and myself, hoping that my hand was not shaking and refraining from any silly comments about this being rather different from London night life. Jess, still with a firm grip on my wrist, was staring intently through the windscreen – possibly wondering if I had installed shatter proof glass. I checked to see that all the windows were closed and locked my door even though it was unlikely that a lion would be familiar with the mechanism of the door handle and its paw would be far too large to fit into the recessed opening in which the handles of older model Land Rovers were housed.

Three or four members of the hyena clan were standing around the carcass staring fixedly at an opening in the surrounding bush – in the shadows we could see others flitting restlessly through the trees. It was a moonlit night and there was no need for the one million candlepower monster torch that lived in the Land Rover's cab.

The first lion emerged from the bush. Reminding me that blood sometimes really does run cold; that the hair on the neck truly does stand up. He was a large male, his enormous head framed by a huge black mane. Penetrating yellow eyes blazed menacingly, the huge mouth hung open to give maximum exposure to those fearsome fangs.

Though he was padding along at a relaxed, easy stroll, there was something about his gait that made it very clear that trying to stop him would be most unwise. A calm but unmistakable message to the hyenas that he was proceeding towards them and that he did not intend to pause.

The message was fully understood by the scavenging clan and one by one the hyenas lost their nerve and retreated towards the trees, some with low, resentful whoops. Moments later, three more males followed in the pawsteps of the first lion and all four gathered around what was left of their dinner.

Not a great deal remained of the kudu and the lions had to work hard to find anything worth eating. The hyenas, meanwhile, circled cautiously, the bolder members of the clan venturing ever closer to the banquet. Like important guests ignoring hovering waiters, the lions continued to search for something of value until one of them felt that the hyenas were becoming too intrusive, too much of a bother. He rose slowly, then darted towards the nearest hyena which retreated as rapidly as its dignity would allow - gambling, no doubt, on the assumption that the lion would not consider a serious pursuit to be worthwhile.

Though heavily outweighed, the hyenas were not prepared to wait patiently for the lions to eat their fill in peace and continued to circle annoyingly, periodic charges from one or other of the lions notwithstanding. Once or twice, with one of the lions in pursuit, they fled right past the Land Rover in that awkward, rolling gait that hyenas have, their smaller, shorter hind legs seeming somehow to be struggling to keep up with the larger, far more powerful front legs.

The lions eventually became bored with the contest, or perhaps they felt that getting a return from the carcass was now becoming too much like hard work. One by one, they rose from the meal and strolled off into the night, the hyenas sending them on their way with triumphant yelps and derisive whoops.

Feeling very humble, I drove the Land Rover slowly back to the camp site. I knew that Jess shared my sentiments and I remarked that I was somehow relieved to have survived the evening with nothing but a slight ache in my left wrist. She refused to believe that she had fastened a circulation stopping grip on it.

I set up the roof-top tent in record time, while Jess nervously swept the area around us with the big torch. Before clambering in record time up to my rooftop haven, I gave her a hug after saying good night. To my great joy she returned my embrace.

Amazing how a few lions can bring people together.

* * *

One can spend days in the bush without seeing a single lion. It had been an unforgettable start to our time in the Okavango.

10

We spent several days roaming around Moremi. The most important decision to be made at the start of each day was where we would spend that night. Once this vital matter had been resolved we would follow the habit of the animals and set off on the day's business at first light, relaxing drowsily in the shade during the mid-day heat. Our aim would be to reach the chosen campsite by late afternoon.

The Okavango is not exactly well signposted and mapping the territory would be a cartographer's nightmare. The roads seem to fan out, then converge, then open out again and then disappear altogether. And the following year would present an entirely different network. We often found ourselves stopping at a fork in the track trying to work out which of several branches we should take. Me squinting up at the sun, doing my best to recall from my army days how to determine where north lay; Jess wearing an only slightly mocking – Well soldier?.... expression.

Asking directions from one of the very infrequently encountered local rangers was an option but one always had to bear in mind that in Africa, the important thing was not so much the directions them-selves, but how to interpret them.

How far was "not far" as opposed to "far-far" – and how many kilometres did a solemn shaking of the head and a low whistle add to the journey?

"Turn left at the first fork then follow that road," seemed straightforward enough but when the first fork offered not two but seven different options one had to give careful thought to the hidden meaning in the words "turn left". Thereafter, following that trail was a simple matter until, a kilometre later, one arrived at the next widely spread fan of options.

While its fun to wander about randomly, one had to bear in mind that the Okavango is not the ideal place in which to get lost – there is no such thing as a search party in this part of the world.

Further, it was wise to fully understand that the location of the nearest petrol station - "far-far" (again that ominous shaking of the head and the whistle) - according to the rangers, could be two hundred kilometres away in an unknown direction. And even long-range tanks eventually run dry.

Somehow though, we managed to find our way, mostly by the road less travelled, and by late afternoon we would arrive at our chosen camp site. Often without seeing another vehicle throughout the day – our only company the rich variety of wildlife found in the delta.

* * *

For me, sunset in Africa is the best time of the day; the time at which The Dark Continent is at its most hauntingly beautiful. A yearning, aching beauty, at once peaceful and serene yet tense and forbidding. A beauty in which the unforgiving Laws of Nature are constantly in operation. Here, life is fragile; violent death ever present.

This peculiar contradiction is at its most poignant as the day draws to a close. While there is a wonderful calm in an African sunset, this is also the start of the dark hours, the time when the lions and the leopards and a variety of smaller predators, come out to hunt. A time of danger, of heightened alertness. In business terms, definitely not a time to be out of stock of any of the senses.

I have always believed that in the bush, the human species is the unwelcome guest of the wild animals. And that we should behave accordingly by respecting their right to what little of the continent we have very generously left to them. My aim, therefore, was always to make the least possible impact on the environment - leaving behind, as someone once put it, only footprints in the sand.

Further, going into the bush was for me an opportunity to forego as many of the trappings of civilisation as possible. To get away from it all rather than to take it all with me. Having oftentimes deviated from the beaten track, I had discovered that less can indeed be more – one can, for example, survive without a solar powered shower, especially when water can be so scarce. An all-over rub with a wet towel can be wonderfully refreshing at the end of a day. And I never understood the point of turning night into day with a blinding gas light that hissed threateningly above its cylinder. There is something magical about dispensing with lights and allowing one's eyes to slowly grow accustomed to the gathering gloom, just as our primitive ancestors would have done centuries ago. And to have thudding music blasting out of several super sub woofer speakers is to obliterate the captivating, mysterious music of an African night.

To my great relief, Jessica shared this view and revelled in this very un-London environment, even checking to make sure I broke none of the rules.

Ours was an archaic viewpoint I know - and a minority one judging by past camping experiences. And it was inevitable that at some stage on our trip, suburbia would come rampaging into the delta.

The invasion began, one night, as a distant roar and our faint hope that it might be a strong wind was soon dispelled. No wind this, it was the sound of a V8 engine being driven hard and it was coming rapidly in our direction. It wasn't long before we were shielding our eyes from the penetrating glare of what must have been about eighteen powerful spotlights mounted on a huge, chrome plated bull bar.

Our hearts sinking, we watched as an enormous Toyota Land Cruiser burst triumphantly into the camp site, circled once or twice in search of a good location, then came to a halt some 20 meters from where I had parked the Land Rover. The lights were doused, the engine turned off and we had the feeling that the two shadowy figures sitting beside the old Land Rover were being viewed with a mixture of amusement and pity. As our eyes gradually recovered, the leviathan came slowly into focus. Outsize BRIDGESTONE tyres bulged aggressively out of gigantic black framed wheel arches. Enormous chrome mirrors protruded from the massive front doors. Mounted on one of the front fenders was a smaller mirror, one that might not survive for long in thick bush, but which could well prove useful in urban shopping centres. One wouldn't want to crush the smaller vehicle parked alongside when reversing out of a parking space. On the rear door an overweight spare wheel covered by a leather case on which was emblazoned in full colour a picture of an eagle. FOUR WHEEL DRIVE proclaimed large lettering on the flanks of the vehicle; lest there be any doubt.

The doors were flung open and, accompanied by a great deal of low, powerful laughter, two men and two women alighted. Someone said something about a rally of the vintage Land Rover Club, a comment greeted by a throaty chuckle and a suppressed giggle.

The driver was a big man, with close cropped hair and a thick neck. A stomach that looked as if it was just beginning to get out of control. Standing there, hands on hips and surveying the camp site, one could see that he was used to giving orders. And having them obeyed. His companion was a large, exceedingly well-endowed woman with a mane of orange hair. Across the front of her straining T shirt in shining sequins were boldly written the words WORLD WRESTLING FEDERATION.

"Goodness me," said Jessica admiringly. "Imagine wrestling with that lot!!"

"Ah yes", I said. "I can see it now. The big guy - writhing in helpless ecstasy - as the Amazon straddles him in the centre of the ring."

I thought it was a rather good image but it earned a sharp slap on the knee from Jess.

"She clad in a tasselled leather bikini and knee-high boots", I added.

"Enough!!" hissed Jessica fiercely.

I refrained from further comment.

The second male, obviously a lesser species, set about gathering what looked like enough firewood to roast an ox while his companion brought out a large folding table on which was placed the inevitable gas light.

"Could that be Springbok Hits Volume 1?" asked Jessica innocently, head cocked on one side, as huge speakers in the back door of the Landcruiser soon destroyed the enchanting music of the African night.

"Should we try to compete with a Brahms symphony?" I asked doubtfully.

11

While our fellow travellers may have been a little insensitive to the privacy of the animals, their hospitality was generous and we were soon gathered around their fire – me helping to make short work of South Africa's National Drink - brandy and coke - while Jess sipped a soft but full-flavoured Merlot

Inevitably the conversation turned to the Okavango and the usual who-saw-what? competition. Jess mentioned our night with the lions and the hyenas adding that even locked in the Land Rover, she had felt a little uneasy.

"What do you say, Dirk?" asked the WWF representative of her partner. Clearly Dirk was an expert on lions. "Wouldn't you have been a bit scared?"

Dirk pulled a packet of Camel from one of several pockets on his bush jacket. He withdrew a cigarette from the pack and, eyes narrowed dangerously, lit it and took a long, hard draw. For a moment I feared that he might suck his entire face down his throat.

Gazing intently into the darkness Dirk spat a shred of tobacco into the fire before delivering his answer.

"I'm not afraid of lions", he announced calmly, little jets of cigarette smoke darting out of his mouth. "I've shot six of them in my time".

The announcement was greeted by several moments of solemn silence.

Jess looked a little sad.

"Shame," the back up to Miss WWF eventually said. "Poor lions".

"What's shame about it?' demanded Dirk. "Every one of those lions had the same chance to get me as I had to get it. That's what hunting is all about".

Jess wore a small, puzzled frown. "Awfully bad luck for the lions that in half a dozen 50/50 contests they failed to register a single victory", she mused innocently, shaking her head slowly.

"What's the most dangerous animal you've ever shot Dirk?" asked the lesser male, thankfully changing the subject. In a low voice he urged that we really should see Dirk's bar back home in Pretoria. The walls, he informed us, shaking his head in admiration, were laden with Dirk's trophies - every one of them a record-breaking specimen. The head of the lion was this big he revealed, hands about a metre apart. This would have made the lion roughly the size of a fully grown ox. Full-colour photographs, we were told, provided irrefutable proof of Dirk's hunting prowess. I imagined Dirk, rifle in hand, posing proudly alongside his vanquished trophies and wondered if his trophy wife was part of the collection.

A long drag on the Camel, a moment's suspense and Dirk tossed back his head to exhale the smoke. He finished with three well formed smoke rings.

"Buffalo", he revealed thoughtfully. "Probably the buffalo".

Clearly an explanation was to follow. We waited in suspense.

"It was at Mana - about four years ago", Dirk recounted. "That's Mana pools in Zimbabwe", he nodded in the direction of Jess and me by way of explanation.

"I was with a rooinek from London – guy out here on some legal business. He'd done a bit of shooting – grouse and pheasant and that", (the tone was only faintly patronising), "and he wanted to get him a buff. Couple of us guys were going up to Zim anyway, so we arranged for the Pom to come with us."

The story was developing excitingly.

"Obviously this guy wasn't that used to the bush", Dirk allowed, "but we walked a bit and eventually we tracked down quite a big herd of buffs". Dirk, of course, would have been a skilled tracker.

"I chose one old bull from the herd – good horns, right shape – and brought this guy into a position where he could get a clear shot.

Told him where to aim – impossible to miss – we'd got right up close". Due no doubt to Dirk's uncanny bushcraft.

A last long drag and the Camel was flicked into the fire.

"Bugger me if the Pom doesn't miss", sighed Dirk, exhaling smoke and shaking his head disbelievingly. "Wounded the bastard".

"You don't want to wound a buffalo", Dirk warned, his tone now business like. "I told the Pom to get the hell behind me, because the buff had now buggered off into thick bush".

Dirk gazed into the fire grimly; it seemed he was back at Mana Pools reliving the incident. We waited in respectful silence for the saga to unfold.

"I knew the buff would have a go at us", Dirk mused. "They're peaceful enough if you leave them alone but they become bloody mean if they're wounded", he continued.

One could sympathise with the buffalo's point of view.

"Anyway, I knew that sooner or later this baby was going to charge and that I probably wouldn't have time to get in a good shot".

"Why didn't you just ..bugger off...with the Pom"? asked WWF's back up.

"You never do that"!! Dirk admonished severely. "You wound an animal, you finish it off"!!

A noble principle.

"Bastard must have circled around behind us somehow", Dirk shook his head in disbelief. It seemed a little unfair really, that a wounded buffalo should outsmart an old hand like Dirk.

"Bastard charged. There wasn't time to aim, I just looked over the sights and pumped off two quick rounds", Dirk continued.

We had to wait while Dirk lit another Camel before the outcome of the action was revealed.

"The bugger's momentum carried him to within less than a yard of where I was standing". Shaking his head and smiling.

Even in the bush, the Laws of Physics are in operation.

"Was it dead?" asked Jessica provocatively.

"You should have seen the Pom", Dirk chuckled, kindly ignoring the question. "Looked as though he'd shat himself".

"Tell them about the leopard Dirk," urged lesser male. It seemed that he acted as some sort of PR agent for the hunter.

Dirk gave a tight little smile. "Clever bastards leopards", he informed the group, staring hard into the darkness . "Work alone and at night, so they're bloody difficult to find".

It seemed like a rather unsporting tactic.

"But I've nailed a couple in my time". Dirk's reputation remained unsullied.

"You should see the leopard skin in front of Dirk's fireplace" lesser male urged me. "Wasn't it a record or something Dirk?"

"It is a big bugger" Dirk had to admit. "But I don't know if it was a record", he shrugged modestly.

"How did you find it?" asked back-up. "Seeing as they're so secretive," she added hastily.

The smoke rings drifted eerily into the night air.

"There's a couple of ways to get you a leopard", Dirk revealed. "But first you have to know that there's one around somewhere in the area. What you do is you get a lamb and tie it to a tree or something in that area. The lamb goes "baa baa" and you know that if its around, the leopard is going to come for that lamb. If you come back and the lamb is gone, you know you're in the right place". Dirk gave a satisfied nod.

"You keep leaving lambs for the leopard, until the bugger gets to know that there's food to be found in that area", he continued. "So one night, you set yourself up in a good place – you look at approach, wind direction – things like that, and you put another lamb out there and it starts baa baa-ing. The leopard comes for the lamb and then there's two ways of doing it".

The denouement was about to be revealed. Dirk smiled at the cleverness of it all as he lit another Camel.

"One - you rig up a light with a rheostat" Exhaling powerfully. "Then, when you hear the leopard taking the lamb, you gradually turn up the light. The leopard thinks it's the moon coming up".

The stupid bastard.

"Or two – and this is the way I prefer. You wait until the leopard has taken the bait then hit it with a spotlight. Of course, the bastard buggers off straightaway, but you've got about half a second to get off a shot".

Way more than enough time for a marksman like Dirk. "That's how I got that one", Dirk inclined his head towards lesser male.

There was a long silence while we digested the ingenuity of it all.

By now, it was getting late and as we planned our usual early morning start we bade our hosts good night. After first asking in which direction they intended to travel.

Then it was off to bed to dream of Dirk effortlessly despatching buffaloes and leopards and prides of record breaking lions.

12

From Moremi we moved northwards into the open grasslands and rocky outcrops of Savuti. There had once been marshlands here but after a series of dry years, they had slowly receded and eventually disappeared altogether.

I thought about asking Jess to tell me a bit about the flora and fauna of those distant times but decided against it.

With a wide range of antelopes, a large giraffe population and huge herds of zebra, it is hardly surprising that the Savuti area is very popular with lions. And during one of our mid-day pauses we were fortunate enough to share a shady copse with one of the resident prides.

The lion is the only species of wild cat that lives in a multi-sex group and while it is the male, with his majestic gold and black mane and arrogant demeanour, who attracts the most admiration, the real power of the pride ultimately lies with the female.

I was sure that Jessica would be aware of this fact and would have brought it to my attention had I not mentioned it.

As she would no doubt be aware, the family nucleus is based on the females − within a pride the lionesses are usually related by birth, be it grandmothers, mothers, daughters, sisters, aunts or cousins. The males on the other hand, may be unrelated one to the other − simply friends who met while cruising around in the bush in their adolescent days. So while the King of the Beasts has an apparently privileged life − sleeping for over twenty hours a day and delegating the tiresome business of hunting to the Queen of the Beasts and her associates − the crown sits uneasily on his head. And the role is not entirely without responsibility.

His task is to protect the pride's territory from bands of roving bachelors. This is where a lusty roar, such as we had heard on our first night in the delta, is a great asset. Its main aim is to make it very clear that this particular turf is already spoken for − that strangers are not welcome. There will always be up-and-coming youngsters eager to test their strength and wrest a territory from the present rulers – and to take over the privileges that being part of a pride bring with them. So an impressive display of roaring sends an unmistakable Keep Out message to strangers.

It is when age creeps up on the King of the Beasts that the insecurity of his tenure becomes apparent. Father Time waits for no lion and the day will come when the strong, young challengers will triumph over the ageing champions. Sometimes in what are little more than very heated verbal exchanges, sometimes in fearful battles in which terrible wounds are inflicted. And then the old will make way for the new – the defeated veterans will slink or limp off to spend what is left of their lives in lonely exile.

This departure is bad news for the cubs of the deposed monarchs. The new king doesn't want the princes of his predecessor hanging around - he much prefers to sire his own cubs. So while the larger male cubs are driven from the safety and comfort of the pride to fend for themselves, for the little ones there is no escape; they are put to the fang by the invaders.

This gruesome infanticide is accepted with equanimity by the females, who, understanding the nature of these things, take a longer term view on the welfare of the pride and submit coyly to the invaders. Somehow, though, they manage to avoid becoming pregnant until they are confident that the newcomers are up to the task of ensuring stability in the pride for the foreseeable future.

"Clever girls," from Jess.

But now, as we watched a tiny cub with a take no prisoners attitude mercilessly plundering the bushy tail of his indulgent father there was no sign of any concern about the dark times that lay ahead for the King of the Beasts.

Retribution, at worst, would come in the form of a lazy cuff, that would send the tiny aggressor rolling through the grass, then scurrying off, ears flat, to less challenging foes like his brothers and sisters.

Watching this relaxed family scene, I thought back to Dirk's comments on what he referred to as his sport and asked Jess if she could help me to understand how one would explain the rules of this particular sport to the lion. This based on the assumption that the word "sport" refers to a contest between two willing participants.

- First, the objective of the hunter. To kill the lion.
- The objective of the lion. To stay alive – preferably without being wounded.
- The hunter would not reveal the venue for the contest, nor the time at which it would start. In fact, the first the lion might know that the game was underway could be when it got a bullet in the head.
- The hunter's weapon – a high powered rifle with all manner of powerful scopes – lethal at several hundred meters.
- The lion would be permitted to use its claws and teeth.
- Under certain circumstances, these same rules would apply, but the lion would be drugged in order to significantly slow down its reactions. This sport would be known as "canned" hunting. Note: The hunter would not be obliged to mention this when giving an account of the game to an admiring audience.

One might find it a little difficult, I suggested, to persuade the lion to take part in the game.

Jess thought for a few moments then shrugged helplessly. "How would I know"? she asked. "I'm just a rooinek from London. And I haven't even shot a pheasant - let alone a grouse."

* * *

We moved on, the next day, to the Linyanti Channel - in many ways a microcosm of the Okavango Delta. Even further off the beaten track, there is a feeling of utter isolation in the Linyanti River forests, a brooding loneliness that brought back a comment made by Trevor when we had celebrated the completion of the restoration project. An observation that it was perhaps a little risky for someone to venture alone into such remote wilderness areas – that two vehicles would definitely be better than one. Flushed with confidence at my newly acquired mechanical proficiency, and absolutely certain that no mishap of any nature would ever befall me, I had not, at the time, given this advice a second thought. How interesting to note, I reflected as we bumped along in a decades old Land Rover, how complacency gives way to a feeling of extreme vulnerability in the remotest corners of the wilderness. More importantly, I had not envisaged having a beautiful lady from London in the passenger seat.

After a couple of hours, the forest gradually gave way to a weary, feeble grassland and it became steadily more difficult to discern the track.

Eventually, the vegetation became so sparse that the track disappeared, initially in places, and then altogether, leaving Jessica and I on the shore of a vast ocean of baked earth with a few scattered islands of disconsolate dry grass and the odd palm tree.

We alighted from the Land Rover and peered anxiously at the hard ground hoping to identify the tell tale signs of a vehicle route. A disturbed sod here, a cracked clod there. To my city slicker eyes, more attuned to scanning sales results and stock sheets, there was nothing to suggest that any vehicle had ever - at any time - passed this way before. I wondered if Dirk, with his special senses, would have been able to make out the way forward. Perhaps to read signs which would enable him to discern not only whether other vehicles had passed this way, but also the brand of tyre, the make of the vehicle, the speed at which it was travelling and the number of average sized adults travelling in it. In much the same way that the San people, those legendary trackers of the old Africa, would have read the multitude of seemingly invisible signs left by passing animals in days gone by.

It was by now mid-morning, a still, cloudless day with not even a gentle breeze to comfort we two anxious travellers. There was no sign of any life, save for a large Marabou stork that studied us gravely – waiting with interest to see how we handled the situation.

Lacking the skills of the bushmen, there was nothing for it but to set off hopefully, avoiding eye contact with the stork. We drove on steadily, a worried silence hanging in the Land Rover's cabin. Humbly, our eyes scanned the parched terrain for any sign a vehicle might have made, in the last ten years, in the infrequent patches of grass. Our ears strained constantly to pick up a missed beat in the steady drone of the old engine - any hint of mechanical malaise or a dried-out cough. Frequent, nervous glances at the Jaeger petrol gauge as the needle swung slowly but surely towards the large E.

Doing my best to appear completely calm and in control, I considered our position. We were very low on both food and fuel, a situation that made losing our way a most unattractive proposition. What to do, I wondered, if the Land Rover spluttered apologeti-cally, jerked once or twice and cut out, the needle coming to rest precisely on that dreaded E? E for Empty. All around us was The Great Nothing – by night, I imagined, we would be in the middle of something akin to a lunar landscape.

I wasn't sure if our stock of food had been exhausted – I had been very happy to leave quarter-mistress duties to Jess but reasoned that to ask what was left at this time might not be good for morale.

Perhaps there was still hope. We had, some time ago, been on a road of sorts. It had been heading in a north-easterly direction. With few obstacles in our path, it seemed that the logical thing would be to continue trustingly in the same direction in the hope that when we reached a more hospitable environment – one in which a faint track might be discerned - we would be lucky enough to pick up the trail.

That would be the logical thing to do, I thought, all the while acutely aware of the fact that in Africa, things are seldom logical.

* * *

By mid-afternoon and with the needle in the petrol gauge flicking ominously over the E, we made out, in the distance, signs of some sort of coastline. The vegetation looked to be less poverty stricken and sparse and gave some hope that we might have crossed this desolate ocean wasteland.

Minutes later, unbelievably, we made out faint tracks in the sparse grass and Jess let out a small sigh as the tracks slowly became a definite trail. I looked across at her with a quizzical expression, as if puzzled by her relief.

"Why the sigh?"

Looking straight ahead she said softly, but with a hint of menace in her voice, "don't go there."

I frowned. "Didn't I tell you that having spent so much time in the bush, I have the power to call on Ancient Spirits?" I asked.

Jess did not reply.

After making our way cautiously along the track for several kilometres we spotted a series of low, ramshackle buildings, one of which carried a chipped enamel sign advertising Coca Cola. A rural store, complete with an old hand operated petrol pump, the likes of which I had last seen at a breathtaking price in an antique shop in Cape Town.

At first sight the settlement appeared to be deserted but to our great relief, it wasn't long before a small band of dusty, barefoot little children emerged from nowhere and gathered around to stare with frank interest at the two interlopers. I smiled winningly at the children, gestured towards the store, and tilted an imaginary bottle to my dry lips - then, pushing my right arm backwards and forwards and with a passable imitation of the noise made by a creaking pump and gushing petrol - filled our empty tank.

Lucky my communication skills were so good. A small messenger wearing a faded Teenage Mutant Ninja Turtles T- shirt sped off into the bush and it wasn't long before an elderly man came ambling towards us. He greeted us with a toothy smile, clapping his hands and chuckling amiably, as though he knew that we were two more or less lost city dwellers who would certainly be boosting his monthly turnover.

We were waved into his surprisingly well-stocked store and were soon sipping ice cold beers that were arguably the most welcome ever consumed by man or woman.

Judging from his prices, the old man was a shrewd shopkeeper who had made more than adequate provision for transport costs to his remote outpost. We spent a good while discussing the economy, the future of his business, life itself – and how it was changing. We shook our heads sadly at the ways of modern youth, agreed wholeheartedly that Man and Womankind had lost their way.

Then, our stores replenished, the petrol tank full, we set off for Chobe.

13

It was late at night and we were sitting in companionable silence in a sandy camp site not far from the Chobe River. Having raised several glasses to the good health of the worthy spirit whose uncanny instinct had guided us so skilfully across the wastelands, a feeling of peaceful somnolence had enveloped us. Jess seemed to be dozing gently in her chair, her hands folded peacefully on her lap. Had she stretched out her arm, she would have been able to touch the four and a half tonnes of African elephant that was tiptoeing politely past her slumbering form.

Only the gentlest rustle of leaves as the giant pachyderm brushed past the tree under which we had made our camp alerted me to its presence. Startled out of my reverie, my first instinct was to yell some sort of warning to Jess but a loud WATCH OUT! seemed inadequate and inappropriate under the circumstances and no suitable alternative came immediately to mind. Instead, I pointed accusingly at the elephant and, spluttering incoherently, half rose out of my chair, spilling the last few drops of my wine. This action awakened Jess; she blinked drowsily, stretched and yawned then focused slowly on me as I at last regained my speech.

"Elephant!" was the best I could eventually manage. Short and to the point but somehow rather inadequate.

Jessica rubbed her eyes sleepily and stared off into the darkness.

"Where?" she asked, absentmindedly reaching for her wine glass.

Even at a relaxed stroll a fully grown elephant, standing almost four metres tall at the shoulder, tends to cover the ground fairly quickly. And quietly. The thick skin that covers its feet works like a giant shock absorber, moulding around rough terrain and enabling the huge creature to move soundlessly over a sandy surface. By now, it would be about thirty metres away.

"Gone", I replied dejectedly.

Jess glanced at the empty glass in my hand but was kind enough not to pass any comment about ancient spirits.

Later, safe in my roof top haven, I ruminated on our close encounter with a member of Africa's largest and most intelligent species. Our visitor had been very big – a fully-grown adult. Perhaps a solitary male - long ago banished from the herd - on the never-ending quest for sustenance? Or perhaps, I mused, our visitor had been the matriarch herself, returning to the herd after an exploratory investigation into the whereabouts of a cherished fruit?

An elephant needs to spend about sixteen hours a day searching for the approximately 135 kilograms of vegetation it requires to keep body and soul together, so in either case there would have been no time to linger at our campsite.

The Chobe area, with its rolling grassy plains and thick mopane woodlands, is home to what little is left of Africa's largest concentration of elephants and in the days that followed, Jess and I were able to experience a remnant of the old Africa – to catch a brief glimpse of what the continent must have been like for elephants before Man discovered that their tusks could profitably be converted into beautifully carved, plump, chortling Buddhas, piano keys, shiny billiard balls and other charming knick-knacks.

At times, sitting quietly in the Land Rover, we were no more than a few metres away from creatures that tipped the scales at around twice the weight of the vehicle – an object that could have been effortlessly rolled over had one of them, on a whim, so fancied.

On one or two occasions we were deemed to constitute a possible threat to the herd, whereupon the senior members would form a protective laager around the calves and, glaring meaningfully at us, spread their enormous ears out wide. This in the belief that by so doing, they would present us with an even more intimidating spectacle - and in this assumption they were entirely correct. A good time, we thought, for us to retire respectfully.

These times reminded me of an incident, many years ago, when a newly married couple enjoying a ride in a game reserve were charged by an enraged elephant. Desperate to escape, the husband, who was at the wheel of their early model Volkswagen beetle, inadvertently changed from first gear to fourth, thereby making it fairly easy for the elephant to keep up with the car and help it on its way with a few good head butts. While the wife was screaming in terror, the husband was apparently laughing hysterically. The elephant, having made its point, then gave up the chase and the couple escaped with little more than a battered rear end to their car. I thought it was a rather amusing tale but Jess looked a little uneasy and seemed not to share my view. (I believe the marriage survived the incident).

Mostly, fortunately, our presence was tolerated and we were able to observe at close quarters the relationships between the various members of the herd with no need to take drastic evasive action.

Elephant society is matriarchal in nature and on the matriarch's enormous shoulders falls the burden of making all decisions, both minor and major, for the family unit. Assuming leadership of a herd is a competitive process and when the time comes for a new leader to emerge the contenders have to demonstrate that they have the wisdom, the authority and the knowledge to effectively lead. So there will be quite a lot of pushing and shoving and loud trumpeting going on as the candidates vie with one another to establish their leadership credentials. Not unlike our own politicians as elections approach but somehow far more civilised and honest.

We observed the great care and attention lavished by mothers and aunts on small calves, some furiously twisting their tiny trunks as though doubtful that these awkward appendages could ever be of any use to them. We watched boisterous adolescent males, continually sparring with each other in their exuberant tests of strength - little knowing that the time would come when their unruly behaviour would lead to the Day of Reckoning - the time when the matriarch, with the support of her senior aides, would go about the unpleasant task of expelling them from the herd. Never again would they be a permanent part of the family unit – their lot from then on would be to wander alone or in small men only groups through the wilderness. Just one of the harsh realities of elephant society.

We were able to eavesdrop on the herd's conversations - an ongoing series of squeaks, grunts and trumpets as matters both trivial and important were discussed. Inaudible to our ears was their infrasonic contact; elephants are able to produce low frequency sounds that enable them to communicate over distances of several kilometres. These signals can travel much further than higher pitched sounds and they are not dissipated by passing through dense forest and woodland.

More than once, we found ourselves subject to the scrutiny of the sad, brooding wisdom in the eyes of the elephants; it was as if they were aware of man and his ways and their unfortunate relationship with him. Through the ages, their strength and intelligence have made elephants ideal candidates for worthy if unwilling service to mankind, both in commerce and in entertainment. Non-unionised Indian elephants have a long and proud history of uncomplaining service in agriculture. Their African cousins have, over the ages, provided mankind with excellent entertainment – be it by fighting to the death with a family member for the amusement of the citizens of the Roman Empire – or, in more benign times, by performing amazing tricks in the circus ring. How very hilarious is the sight of elephants - pink, cone-shaped hats stuck on their heads, balancing on small stools! I hoped that no descendant of any of the luckless creatures I had giggled at in childhood visits to the circus was a member of this herd.

Some express great concern about the apparently wanton destruction of the environment by elephants in the Chobe (and other) areas and we couldn't help but notice that large areas had indeed been laid waste. With a profligacy usually shown only by the human species, the elephants looked to be waging war on the environment – pushing down trees for no apparent reason and stripping bark, seemingly with no intention of ever consuming it. Those who lament this so-called destruction would, however, do well to acknowledge that in the days when there were far more elephants and far fewer humans, the bush was in much better condition than it is now.

Nor should we too swiftly (and arrogantly) judge the ways of Mother Nature; many naturalists have noted that this apparently destructive activity is an integral part of the on-going process of the regeneration of the bush lands. The removal of trees creates browse for shorter animals and the process can make way for new, more nutritious grasslands providing sustenance for the likes of zebra, wildebeest and other grazers. And the elephants might add, in their defence, that their actions are partly a consequence of the destruction by man of so much of their own habitat.

Perhaps too, the ruthless and continuing elimination of the finest members of their society is to some extent responsible for this seemingly destructive behaviour. The size of tusks is obviously a key factor in deciding which trophy to choose – the bigger the tusks, the better. The Dirks of this world have no interest in tusks of modest proportions and this, of course is bad news for the tuskers – the large bulls and the matriarchs with their magnificent, sweeping tusks. It is possible, given the place that the large elephants have in their society, that their elimination has a profound and traumatic effect on the herd.

One must, many scientists would have us believe, steer well clear of any leanings towards anthropomorphism. But knowing a little about elephant society and having spent several days among the elephants, Jess and I would have been hard pushed to assert that these most intelligent of mammals feel none of the emotions we humans experience. Several observers have noted the difficulty elephants seem to experience in accepting the death of a family member and the sorrow that such an event so obviously brings. And it would have been difficult for us to argue, watching the obvious pleasure that members of the herd experienced when greeting each other, trunks intertwined, that what they were feeling was not something akin to our own feelings of joy on such occasions.

* * *

Like so many creatures in Africa, the elephant faces an uncertain future. While the rampant poaching that accounted for an estimated three quarters of a million elephants during the 1980s is now partly under control, the poaching continues. And the rapid growth of the human population – and the consequent destruction of the elephants' habitat – have had far more serious implications for the future of these magnificent animals.

With this sombre thought in mind, we bade farewell to the Chobe tuskers and, having negotiated the border post at Kazungula, were soon rolling along the road to the Victoria Falls.

14

Though "the smoke that thunders" had long been known to the local inhabitants, it was only in the late 1850s that this majestic panorama was revealed to the outside world. While Dr. David Livingstone, possibly the first white man to set eyes on the falls, was later to speak kindly of their beauty, asserting that "Scenes so beautiful must have been gazed upon by angels in their flight," the missionary/explorer must have experienced mixed feelings when he first gazed upon the spectacle. A waterfall almost two kilometres long and more than one hundred metres high was not a welcome sight for one who had long cherished an ambition to use the Zambezi as a navigable trade route between the coast and the interior. Livingstone abhorred slavery and believed that the best way to counter it was to open up the hinterland to commercial trade. But not even with his indefatigable energy and determination could the good doctor find a way for his boats to navigate such an obstacle. One that, in full flood became an avalanche of seething, boiling, fury - obliterated from sight by a dense, drenching spray. Mosi oa tunya – the smoke that thunders.

After uncomplainingly carrying Jessica and I some three thousand kilometres over some of the most inhospitable terrain in Africa I felt that the Land Rover was entitled to a well-deserved service. As luck would have it there was in the Victoria Falls village a garage owned by a man who could have been a Zimbabwean version of Trevor.

Thoroughly familiar with the more senior models, Rob was happy for me to assist in the work – my having very modestly told him of my involvement in the restoration of the vehicle.

I asked Jess if she would like to join us – or, if she trusted us to handle the service – she might like to hire a car and take a drive around the environs. Somewhat to my relief, she chose the latter.

On the morning of the service, we made our way to one of the car hire companies in the Falls village. We entered a large, spotlessly clean office with the mandatory larger than life size photograph of President Robert Gabriel Mugabe prominent on the back wall.

"Good morning sah". Beauty Sibanda greeted us with a smile as wide as the Victoria Falls and brighter than the sun above it. Immaculate in her red and white uniform she positively radiated good cheer.

Having assured Beauty that all was well with me and Jessica — and our families - and had confirmation that things could not possibly be better in her home - I informed Beauty that Jess would like to rent a car for the day.

Beauty obligingly tendered a plastic-coated chart on which was printed a long list of vehicles and the daily, weekly and monthly rates of hire.

"Hmm", I mused, studying the list.

"Why don't you go for the Jaguar?" I asked Jess.

Beauty's yell of laughter was infectious. Covering her mouth with one hand she slapped an ample thigh with the other while turning to face her several colleagues hard at work at their desks in the spacious office behind her. They all joined Beauty in her mirth. Jess smiled broadly.

"Oh no, sah — we got no Jaguar!" Beauty explained as the laughter subsided.

"O.K. Jess" I went on. "What about…umm…hey, look at this — a Range Rover Vogue!?"

This proposal, it seemed, was even funnier than the first one. Covering her face with both hands, Beauty, bent almost double, took several backward steps, while her colleagues clapped delightedly, nodding vigorously to one another. By now, Jess had joined in the laughter, clapping along with Beauty's colleagues.

Recovering her composure, Beauty returned to the counter.

"We got no Range Rover, sah", she explained, dabbing her eyes with a white handkerchief.

Beauty waited expectantly, her smile broader than ever.

"Beauty" Jess asked when calm had returned to the office. "What do you have?"

Beauty now became very serious. Frowning fiercely, she looked hard at the list, then jabbed a finger at an entry.

"We got a Mazda," she eventually disclosed.

"Fine Beauty," Jess replied with a friendly smile. "Fine. I'll take the Mazda".

"Ah...yes".

We could tell from the worried frown on her face that something was troubling Beauty.

"There is one problem" she revealed gravely. "The Mazda is at the airport". The airport was about 20 kilometres from the village.

We considered this conundrum for a few moments.

"Any chance.... you could have it brought to the village?" Jess eventually enquired.

"Ah...yes", was Beauty's answer but we noticed that the frown did not leave her face. "I will phone the airport".

Beauty returned to her desk and dialled a number on her phone. A lengthy conversation followed - it seemed that bringing the car to the village was not going to be a straightforward matter.

Eventually, Beauty put down and phone and returned to the counter.

"Ah...there is one problem," she disclosed sorrowfully. "We cannot find the driver". Disappointed sighs, sorrowful shaking of the heads from her colleagues.

We thanked Beauty for her wonderfully friendly service and wished her well. The bright smile was back on her face; the mood of good humour restored in the office.

There was another car rental office on the opposite side of the road. I pushed open the door.

A smartly dressed gentleman immediately left his desk and met us at the counter. Whereas Beauty had been the essence of familiar, friendly welcome, this approach was more formal, more serious.

"Good morning sir", the greeting accompanied by a vigorous nodding of the head. Patrick Nyandoro - proclaimed a brass name plate on his spotless white shirt.

After exchanging the usual polite greetings, I asked if Patrick might have a car to rent?

Patrick carefully studied a blackboard resting against the wall – on it were written in chalk details of several vehicles. After a few moments, he politely excused himself and disappeared into a back office, emerging moments later with someone who was obviously the senior manager in the operation.

"Good morning." Thomas Ndhlovu's handshake was firm.

Together Thomas and Patrick studied the list, occasionally murmuring quietly to each other as we waited in respectful silence. Eventually, a conclusion was reached.

Thomas approached the counter - leant forward over it with a conspiratorial air. I looked briefly at Jess, then over my shoulder to make sure we were not being watched, then joined him - my elbows on the counter, one hand shielding my face.

Thomas lowered his voice. "We got one car," he revealed. "A Mazda. But there is a problem".

I waited with bated breath.

"It is at the airport".

We parted on the best of terms. "Not to worry", I said as Jess and I walked towards the door. "Thank you very much."

"Looks like a quiet day at the pool for you", I said to Jess.

15

I met Jess at the motel late that afternoon, having enjoyed working with Rob on my first Land Rover service. Her eyes were shining. "I met a guy at the pool this afternoon."

I blinked once or twice. "I hope you'll be very happy together."

Jess laughed. "Hello, hello!! It's like that, is it?"

She explained. "He organises canoe safaris down the Zambezi. Starting at a place called Chirudu or something and finishing at Mana Pools."

I hoped that my face did not betray the sense of immense relief that I felt.

There had been a cancellation, Jess went on; a two-person canoe was available. "Can we go?"

I could find no objection to this proposal, though I hoped that the buffalo herd that had been deprived of its leader by Dirk's deadly rifle would have forgotten the incident by now.

I met Des later that night at the camping site's bar and we signed on for the trip. I would ask Rob if we could leave the Landie in his workshop for a week or so and we would travel with Des in his truck – through Zambia to Chirundu – where we would meet up with the rest of the group and set off for Mana Pools. Departure time was first thing to-morrow morning.

So it was that early the following day, we crossed the beautiful Victoria Falls bridge into Zambia and set off for Chirundu.

Des was a big man, with the lean, hard look of one who would be able to survive in the bush for days on end, living off the land; quite happy with his own company. On one brawny shoulder was a bold tattoo – a skull with the head of what looked like a Gaboon viper protruding menacingly from one empty eye socket. One imagined that Des would be pretty handy with a gun and a knife – in fact, he could probably strip any weapon - even in complete darkness - behind his back. A regular soldier in one of the elite units of the South African army, he had taken early retirement when the foolish war in Angola had ended and had drifted into selling security systems. But he had never been one to be confined to an office and it had not been long before his company had let him go and he had taken off in search of adventure. He had found freedom in the form of canoe safaris down the Zambezi.

While I had been an unwilling conscript rather than a regular soldier, Des and I were later to discover that our travels had taken us to some of the same remote destinations. I had not particularly enjoyed my army days and was reluctant to talk about them – a reticence that Des mistook for the professional soldier's unspoken rule never to discuss (unless in very esoteric company), one's army experiences. But Des' eyes narrowed and he gave a small, understanding smile. From now on, I could see, we would communicate with hand signals and nods. Having told Jess of my lack of enthusiasm for army life, I noticed that her eyes were shining dangerously and there was a small but wicked grin on her lips and sensed that she understood that Des and I were not quite in the same league when it came to waging war. I wondered if she still recalled my observation that she snored gently and hoped she would not contrive some innocent way to gain revenge by revealing the misapprehension.

To my relief, Jess held her tongue.

Skilfully avoiding the bomb crater-like potholes in the Great North Road, Des made good time through Zambia and by late afternoon, having re-entered Zimbabwe through the border post at Kariba, we were installed in the small hotel at Chirundu. The term "heavy traffic" in this tiny border post can describe either an excess of five cars on the road at the same time, or a large elephant. Here, a man riding his bicycle down one side of the road would barely notice an elephant plodding along down the other side. So it was no surprise that the waiter at the hotel complained that the adolescent elephant slaking its thirst from the hotel swimming pool had become a bit of a nuisance. We raised our glasses to the youngster and drank to her health.

At nine 'o'clock the following morning, we were on the banks of the Zambezi River, being introduced to our fellow paddlers. There were eight of us in all – including Des. His eyes steely, he briefed us on what lay ahead.

The trip to Mana Pools would take four days, so we would spend three nights camping by the river. We would be brought back to Chirundu by truck. Paddle in single file, Des instructed, and don't get too close to the other canoes - except for the very popular "leg-overs" – when we linked canoes to have a cold beer. Do not put a hand or a foot into the river while paddling. Apparently crocodiles could be waiting hopefully for just such opportunities. Where possible, we would overnight on islands in the Zambezi, but when on the mainland, we were not to stray far from the canoes. Affectionately patting his rifle, Des explained that a great deal of tiresome paperwork was necessary if he had to use the weapon. And he hated having to write reports.

We could wade into the river to wash – but, Des suggested, no deeper than the ankles. We were free to swim if we wanted to but if one of us should lose an arm to a crocodile – as had happened to another canoeist recently – we were, he pointed out, a long way and many hours from the nearest hospital. And when we left our camp sites, Des let it be known, we should leave nothing behind. He would make sure, he told us smilingly, that no-one had forgotten anything like an empty bottle or a piece of waste paper. Des had clearly learnt a little diplomacy since his army days.

Our biggest danger, he revealed, would be the many hippos we would encounter along the way. While most animals would tolerate our presence, we would not try to get close to the likes of, for example, an elephant in musth, a lioness with new-born cubs, a rhino with some sort of injury. Understandably, the presence of human beings would not be welcome under such circumstances. But hippos could be unpredictable and aggressive for no particular reason and where we were headed, the odds were stacked, literally, very heavily in their favour.

Indemnity forms duly signed, we packed what few possessions and provisions could be accommodated in the canoes and pushed off into the wide Zambezi. The canoes were broad-bottomed and stable and going with the downstream flow, we were soon paddling serenely past woodlands of acacia and leadwoods, mahogany and raintrees, with frequent sightings of elephant, buffalo and zebra and a wide variety of antelope. And, of course, hippos.

For hippos, the fun part when dealing with canoeists is the ability to play hide and seek. They could watch us, just their bulbous eyes and small ears above the surface, then disappear with a loud sigh. They could then choose a spot, any spot, to burst triumphantly to the surface – often with a loud expulsion of air and perhaps a deafening honk-honk. And possibly twenty or so metres closer to the line of canoes. Having studied the effect that this ominous action had on the paddlers, the hippos could again sigh and with a mean-ingful glare, sink beneath the surface. Where, one wondered, would they next surface? Another twenty metres closer to the canoes? Perhaps underneath one of them? Des laughingly told us of an inci-dent on one of his safaris when a hippo had come up under a canoe and its occupant had become only the second man in history to walk on water. We assumed, because of Des' levity, that the man had survived.

Later, as we paddled slowly down the river, I told Jess a charming children's tale recounted around the fire in Africa. It concerns, I explained the habit that hippos have of opening their enormous mouths very wide from time to time as they float in the river. Long ago, the story goes, hippos were land animals condemned, because of their sensitive skins, to suffer in the sun. So a delegation of senior hippos was sent to petition Ngozi to allow hippos to spend the daylight hours in the water. Not surprisingly, Ngozi was apprehensive about this request, fearing that with their enormous appetites the hippos might become fish eaters and very quickly empty the rivers of all fish. So he refused the plea. The hippos persisted, however, and eventually, a compromise was reached. They would be allowed to spend time in the river – but only during the day when it was hot. At night, they were to leave the river and continue with their vegetarian diet. And during the day, the hippos had, every now and then, to open their huge mouths as widely as they could, to prove to Ngozi that they had not yielded to temptation and sampled a fish or two.

A charming little story – but less so when one is in a light-weight canoe just twenty metres from this declaration of innocence. Another theory, we would later agree, could be that hippos enjoy displaying their fearsome tusks before canoeists to show them what they could expect should there be any sort of conflict. The prospect of two tonnes of irritated hippo surfacing under one's canoe would be for us sufficient incentive to forget any fatigue or stiffness and respond immediately to Des' exhortations to hurry past those individuals known to be of a foul disposition.

Our passage would be marked by loud honks from the hippos – it seemed that they had some form of early warning system for their associates downstream and at the first sign of our presence, those basking on the banks would plunge into the water. For some reason that is difficult to understand, huge hippos feel very vulnerable on dry land and much prefer the sanctuary of water when they feel threatened – even by feeble humans in fragile canoes. This probably accounts for the toll hippos have taken of human lives – getting between a hippo and water is not a good situation to be in and many a local unfortunate enough to be at the riverside has been flattened by a hippo in a frantic hurry to get back to the safety of the water.

Almost as if to demonstrate this, as we rounded a bend in the river one panic-stricken hippo broke cover from the grass and belly-flopped into the river just a couple of metres in front of our canoe –

our desperate back-paddling almost lifting the canoe out of the water. No time to assure the beast that we meant it no harm – that we wanted only to pass by peacefully.

As our heart beats slowly returned to normal, Jess turned around to fix me with an accusing stare as though I was somehow to blame for the incident. I felt it would be unkind to remind her that it was she who had wanted to come on the canoe expedition. So I politely suggested that she keep an eye on what lay ahead, both in the river and on the bank, lest another hippo suddenly made a dash for the safety of the water. I think my sweet little hippo tale had been forgotten.

* * *

Des had an encyclopaedic knowledge of the flora and fauna of the area and, it seemed, the eyesight of an eagle. "Bateleur", pointing to a tiny speck in the sky. "Immature male". And an ability to spot objects invisible to the urban eye. "Croc", inclining his head slightly towards the bank as a gentle ripple 30 metres downstream gave away the sinister entry into the water of a four metre long crocodile. We picked daintily at the water with our paddles, keeping our hands well above the surface.

Our first night was to be spent on a small, sandy island about midway between Zambia and Zimbabwe. Little more than a large sandbank, it had no trees or grass and as we would be sleeping right out in the open, we were glad of our well insulated sleeping bags squeezed into the bows of the canoe. While winter days on the Zambezi River are wonderfully warm and sunny, the temperature can drop significantly during the night.

Not unexpectedly, Des was an expert fisherman and an accomplished chef, turning our modest rations into a veritable feast. As self-appointed representatives of the Cape Winelands, Jess and I had managed to make room for a small number of wines in our canoe and a flinty Zambezi river-cooled Sauvignon Blanc proved to be the perfect complement for Des' freshly caught bream. Could there, we wondered as we sat around the fire gazing in silent awe at the spectacular sunset, be a more agreeable place to be?

The sun disappeared rapidly below the tree line – a signal for the music of the African night to begin. The call of a nightjar. The mournful whoo..oop of a hyena. A sudden startled trumpet from an elephant. Then that unmistakeable groan of a lion.

Huddled against each other for the cold, Jess laid her head on my shoulder and gave a deep sigh.

16

We were awoken in the middle of the night by total pandemonium. The ground was shaking, there was a deafening drumming noise and what sounded like a great deal of splashing. All punctuated by what I realised was the panic-stricken trumpeting of what must have been a large herd of elephants.

I contemplated the situation. If those elephants were coming our way, we had but seconds to live. No point trying to extricate ourselves from our sleeping bags and make a run for it.

Here lie the remains of Denis Shirley and Jessica Barnard. Totally flattened by a herd of panicking elephants. RIP.

Fortunately the drumming gave way to splashing, the trumpeting ceased. Then silence.

"Elephants", Des remarked sleepily. "Must have swum across to the island and been spooked by our scent when they arrived. Go back to sleep".

After what could well have been our last night on earth, we set off early the next morning.

Most canoe safaris on the Zambezi are confined pretty much to paddling along fairly close to the river bank but Des had a special permit that allowed him – with his rifle – to venture away from the river and into the bush on foot. When we took a break, after paddling for a couple of hours that morning, Des asked if anyone would care to join him for a stroll into the wilds. The rest of the party wisely declined but Jess and I immediately put our hands up.

Having, on a couple of occasions, had the good fortune to observe an excellent tracker at work, I was again to be amazed at the tracker's art.

"Duiker" – pointing to a slightly bent slip of grass. "A while back".

"Hyena. Probably a small male," pointing to nothing in particular on the ground. "Yesterday".

And then - this time in a more serious tone - "elephant. Very large - probably a male. Recent… like a few minutes."

Suddenly, I wondered if it had been such a good idea for Jess and me to take a stroll in the bush. This had quickly become one of those "it seemed like a good idea at the time" moments. One would do well to remember that wild animals are wild. And that if in musth, a large male can be somewhat unpredictable and capricious.

Here comes that humble, vulnerable feeling again.

We hadn't walked more than a few hundred metres when we saw the owner of the footprints. Des had correctly divined that the elephant was large. Very large. And plodding along no more than about fifty metres ahead of us. It was a male and – in all probability - in musth

Matters had, rather suddenly, taken a somewhat unfortunate turn. What, I wondered, were we doing here right now? Three very small creatures, very exposed, in the African bush – uncomfortably close to a large elephant. Where was the Land Rover when we needed it?

Des held up his hand. In a low voice he instructed us – "remember – an elephant can run very much faster than we can. If he charges, whatever you do, don't run. Just stand very still."

Sure Des. No problem. I won't run. I'll just stand very still. I wondered if I would be able - should the elephant decide to charge us – to just stand very still.

Rather than try my luck by running away.

We didn't have long to consider the options.

Without any warning - and for no apparent reason, (perhaps Jess or I had trodden on a dry twig) - the huge pachyderm suddenly swung around – and, accelerating horribly - came hurtling towards us, trumpeting in an enraged manner, ears flapping widely, trunk pointing menacingly at us. Jess seized my arm but, somehow, neither of us disobeyed Des' command to stand very still. Probably because the sight of more than four tonnes of infuriated elephant seemingly bent on our total destruction tends to freeze one's reactions.

With breath-taking speed the enormous animal thundered ever nearer while Des, peering over the rifle he had instantly tucked into his shoulder repeatedly yelled HEY!! HEY!! HEY!! in a defiant, authoritative way.

Lucky he spoke a bit of elephant, I thought.

Just as it seemed that we would be run over by the furious animal, the great beast shuddered to a sudden halt, raising a huge cloud of dust. It turned side on and shaking its massive head as though it just could not understand the stupidity of the pathetic creatures cowering fearfully before it, turned around and slowly walked away.

"Mock charge" said Des calmly, lowering his rifle. "They do that sometimes".

Clearing my throat, lest I squeak and doing my best to speak in an enquiring, academic sort of way, I asked how one could tell the difference between a mock charge and a real one. Des looked at me in what I thought was a rather patronising way.

"With a mock charge, the elephant stops just before it flattens you".

A few moments while we digested this seemingly obvious answer.

"And…. when does one know if the elephant is going to stop…. or flatten you?" Jess asked respectfully in a small voice.

"Instinct tells you".

We left it at that.

Let's go back to the classroom for a moment and ponder the physics. How far would the impetus of a well above average size elephant, travelling at, what seemed to me, about 120 k.p.h., carry it if Des' instinct had told him that this was not a mock charge, but a real one and he had pulled the trigger? While I was never very good at physics, I imagined it would be a bit further than the five or so metres that separated us from the elephant when it decided to make this one a mock charge rather than a real one.

Our appetite for a walk in the bush having very quickly left us, we suggested to Des that we should perhaps – selflessly – return to the river to check on the other members of the safari lest they start to worry about us.

We found them paddling a little nervously in the shallows of the Zambesi.

"See anything?" they asked.

"Nothing", Jess replied.

Our last night was spent at Mana Pools. By now we all felt that we had paid our school fees to the wild – that we had been through some sort of African wildlife initiation ritual. Gazing sleepily into the dying embers of our fire, tales of our various experiences already growing fast in the telling, our last bottle of Shiraz drained, we crept into our sleeping bags, moved them a little closer to the fire and fell asleep.

I will never know if I dreamed about that hyena or if it was real. I seem to remember waking up and looking into its face which, it seemed, was less than a metre from mine. It was crouching down and staring intently at me. I think it had rather bad breath. Not wanting to be unkind, I waved my hand at it and muttered something like "go away" – quietly, lest I disturb the others. Des might have said something more forthright.

I mentioned the matter to him next morning – he told me of a case where a hyena had taken a large chunk out of someone's face under circumstances very similar to mine. I don't know if he was keeping something from me.

Having promised sincerely to keep in touch, we bade farewell to our fellow travellers. Then we set off with Des on the return journey to the Victoria Falls looking forward to a happy reunion with the Land Rover - the trusty vehicle, well-rested and serviced - would no doubt be eager to move on.

* * *

When (with my semi-invited guest) I had set off from Cape Town, I did not have a clear idea of where I would go. The Okavango was the first destination, then Chobe, then the Vic Falls - but thereafter?

Decision time had come.

Back in the Victoria Falls camping site, and fully relaxed after several cold beers we discussed the situation with Des. Where to now? Without going into sensitive details of his army career, it was clear that he had travelled well outside the borders of South Africa. There was a far-off look in his eyes.

"Serengeti", he murmured – almost to himself. "Ngorongoro. The Mara."

Jess blinked. "You're talking… would that be…. Uganda? Aren't those places….quite a long way from here?"

"Sure," Des replied. "Those places are in Tanzania and Kenya actually, so of course you would need the right vehicle. Which you have." After an appraising look at the Landie. Des would of course be familiar with the vehicle's capability.

From the compartment in the driver's door of the vehicle I fetched a map of Southern Africa – already worn and soiled enough to suggest honourable service.

"From here to… would it be Nakonde…? would be about … 1,500 kilometres" I speculated.

"About right" Des confirmed. "That would take you to the border of Tanzania."

Then there would be a few more kilometres to the Serengeti. And another couple to the Maasai Mara.

"There are some worthwhile reserves in Zambia," Des ventured.

"Luangwa, Kafue – both worth a visit on your way if you have the time."

One more for the road and then it was to bed.

* * *

I thought long and hard and late into the night about our situation. Our time in the bush had been wonderful and uplifting and I felt no need to set off on the return journey to Cape Town.

But I had no idea of Jessica's situation – or how much time she had to spare. In my view, no places better represented the dangerous beauty of Africa than Kenya and Tanzania. I had paid fleeting visits to both the Serengeti and the Maasai Mara – and the Ngorongoro crater – while on business, but always with the vow to return. Perhaps now was the time? I certainly had little enthusiasm for following up with those employment agencies which had told me they would be back to me the very second that something suitable came up.

But what of Jess? I realised that I had, in the time that we had spent together, become more than a little fond of her. I couldn't bear the thought of putting her on a plane to South Africa. We had not once spoken of her return to England and I knew nothing of her work commitments, or how much time she had on her hands.

* * *

After a full monty type breakfast at that wonderful colonial relic the Victoria Falls Hotel, Des asked what our next move would be.

"I think I can hear the Great North Road calling," I told him.

At a time when the Sun Never Set on the British Empire the vision of a highway – The Great North Road - that ran from the Cape colony to Cairo without ever passing out of British held territory was thought to be not only right and proper, but rather splendid. Starting in the Union of South Africa, the road would run through first Southern, then Northern Rhodesia, on through Tanganyika, Kenya and the Sudan and finally, triumphantly, into Egypt. An ambitious undertaking – some 10,000 kilometres through the very heart of the Dark Continent. The first successful attempt to undertake the journey, in 1924 - 26, took one year and four months; another attempt - some ten years earlier - had come to an unfortunate end when the leader of the expedition had been killed by a leopard in Rhodesia.

We bade a fond farewell to Des – asked him to send our best regards to the hippos and remember us to the angry bull elephant. Waved until his battered old truck was out of sight.

I had not been able to broach the subject of Jessica's return to England. But the dreaded moment had now come.

"I think it's the Great North Road for me," I told Jess. "But I guess you'll be wanting to head back to England. Perhaps we should see if we can put you on a plane for South Africa?"

We went into the hotel and found the travel desk. Yes, there was a plane to Johannesburg that morning. And yes, there were a couple of seats available.

Well. That's it. Looks like the time to say goodbye has come. (Violins playing softly in the background).

I looked at Jess. To my great dismay, there were tears in her beautiful brown eyes.

"Damn you," she said. "This was not supposed to happen."

I shrugged and shook my head in a - Now What Have I Done Wrong? way. Waited for some kind of explanation.

Jess wiped away her tears.

"The reason I came back to South Africa was not really to see family," she said sorrowfully. "It was because a long relationship had come to an end. When I found out that my partner – my life and business partner – had been having an affair. Right under my nose."

She shook her head angrily. "What a sordid, silly little story."

"Life's like that," were about the wisest words I could come up with. Rather inadequate I know.

'I left England promising myself that I would never allow the same thing to happen again. That I would take a long break from relationships – then start again. As a wiser woman."

"Makes sense," I ventured cautiously.

Jess looked away.

"So when my stupid brother suggested that I go with you on your great breakaway adventure, I thought it would be the perfect opportunity to get away from it all".

"Then what happens?" she asked.

It was a rhetorical question, I sensed - and I did not have an answer.

"I fall in love with you."

She put her hands to her eyes, which were again filling with tears.

"What a fool I am!!" she exclaimed angrily.

I put my arms around her.

"That must make two of us," I said. "Because I have loved you from the very first moment I saw you."

Jess pulled back with a start. Looked hard at me with those lovely eyes.

Then threw her arms around my neck.

"Bastard!!!" With great feeling.

She freed herself from my arms. Strode out of the hotel to the Land Rover, climbed into the driver's seat.

"Where's the Great North Road?" she asked. "I'm driving."

EPILOGUE

"We do not inherit this Land from our Parents;
   We borrow it from our Children."

Ralph Waldo Emerson? A Native American observation?

I had sometimes wondered how much, in terms of wildlife, I had inherited from my parents. And what I would bequeath to my children when my race was run. No-one knows for sure how many of the Big Five - lions, elephants, buffalos, leopards and rhinos - roamed Southern Africa when I was born. Nor how many species of butterflies and flowers existed at that time. All that is known for certain, is that my generation will continue the fine tradition of leaving to its children a great deal less than it inherited from its parents.

It would seem that, very sadly, the sun is setting on The Big Five. And a great deal more.

Compared to many other parts of the world, the demolition job in southern Africa was commenced fairly recently. Four hundred years ago, the southern part of the continent was inhabited by relatively simple Man. The San people had dominated the hinterland of southern Africa for some 10,000 years - living a nomadic existence in near perfect harmony with their environment. Taking from Nature only what they needed. A hunter-gatherer lifestyle that withered away before the advance of the black and white races.

How beautiful it must have been. As a youngster, I had read many books by authors like Frederick Courteney Selous, one of Africa's more famous Great White Hunters, who had tramped through the bush in the late 1800s shooting everything in sight. Fortunately, Selous was a naturalist as well as a hunter, so he conscientiously recorded the details of all the animals he slaughtered and carefully described the paradise that existed – even then - in southern Africa at that time. Reading his accounts, it is very difficult, now, to imagine the vast numbers of creatures that roamed the southern part of the continent in those days; the forests and plains that stretched as far as the eye could see.

The arrival of the curiously named "civilised man", of course, spelled the beginning of the end for Africa's Garden of Eden. Early traders and hunters worked tirelessly and unceasingly at shooting any animal with commercial value – and a good many others either on a whim or in the name of "sport". It was unfortunate too, that in the pursuit of feeding themselves, (on crops grown by humans – after they had slashed and burned the original graze), the animals had suddenly been classified as pests or vermin and had, therefore, to be shot. Impatient and less willing to understand than the original dwellers, civilised man preferred to force Nature's systems into directions more suited to his own immediate needs. And as Africa's human population steadily grew and then exploded, as farmlands spread, as factories were built and habitats destroyed - Africa's flora and fauna retreated to ever shrinking areas until, for many species, it was the end of the road.

Sadly, in a supposedly more enlightened era, the depredation has not ended. Millionaires pay vast sums to shoot anything from a lion (drugged or otherwise), to a giraffe and desperately poor people are paid what for them is a fortune to poach rhinos. This so that their horns can be used by eastern witchdoctors to apparently cure all manner of ills and inadequacies. (Thanks are due here to Mother Russia's gift eternal to Africa – the ubiquitous AK 47).

Despite the magnificent and heroic efforts of many conservation bodies and warnings from several respected sources, "development" rushes on unabated. No matter how well motivated the warnings from those concerned about the destruction of the environment, there can always be found counter arguments. Where there are large profits to be made, it is always possible to produce impressive scientific reports that prove conclusively and beyond doubt, that turning over yet another few hundred hectares of pristine natural vegetation to a championship golf course and five hundred exclusive, up-market homes with superior finishes would, in fact, have little impact on the ecosystem. Little - if any at all.

Generously, certain areas have been set aside as sanctuaries for what remains of the wild animal population, though unfortunately, all that could be spared in South Africa was around 4% of the total land area. And even here, the wildlife would, of course, have to pay its way through tourism, hunting and culling – increasingly, for the mega rich.

Africa's great heritage is its wildlife. How very sad if a time should come when Denis and Jess could no longer roam around what little is left of the wilderness. If the only places where one could find the Big Five would be in what are little more than giant zoos which do not allow many species to live their natural, ages-old lives.

THE END

www.ingramcontent.com/pod-product-compliance
Lightning Source LLC
Chambersburg PA
CBHW061138200626
46817CB00016B/1978